TAMED BY T

Doms of Destiny, Colorado 5

Chloe Lang

MENAGE EVERLASTING

Siren Publishing, Inc.
www.SirenPublishing.com

A SIREN PUBLISHING BOOK
IMPRINT: Ménage Everlasting

TAMED BY TEXANS
Copyright © 2014 by Chloe Lang

ISBN: 978-1-62741-012-0

First Printing: April 2014

Cover design by Les Byerley
All art and logo copyright © 2014 by Siren Publishing, Inc.

ALL RIGHTS RESERVED: This literary work may not be reproduced or transmitted in any form or by any means, including electronic or photographic reproduction, in whole or in part, without express written permission.

All characters and events in this book are fictitious. Any resemblance to actual persons living or dead is strictly coincidental.

Printed in the U.S.A.

PUBLISHER
Siren Publishing, Inc.
www.SirenPublishing.com

DEDICATION

To Mr. Blissful, husband to my wonderful friend, Sophie. He's always ready to listen to me and answer my questions about the publishing industry and marketing.

Thank you, Rich, for your friendship and support.

And

To the dear readers at Righteous Perverts and The Naughty Book Club. Your support and enthusiasm is greatly appreciated.

TAMED BY TEXANS

Doms of Destiny, Colorado 5

CHLOE LANG
Copyright © 2014

Chapter One

Jena Taylor hit the send button and smiled. "Who says crime doesn't pay?"

She shifted in her chair. Four hours of coding had made her shoulders tight. Stretching, she looked around the large expanse of the warehouse.

I would've never dreamed I'd be in Odessa, Texas.

It was already past six o'clock. How much money was Scott Knight willing to spend?

Apparently, quite a lot.

This was the seventh control room he'd set up for her. She'd estimated the funds it took to get all this equipment to be more than one hundred thousand dollars. It had to be more than a million in all the locations.

Going legit felt great, especially with the kind of bankroll Knight had.

Time to relax.

She sipped on her coffee. Just a few more tasks and then she could get some much-needed rest back at her hotel.

She'd dreamed of being on this kind of project since leaving MIT and escaping Carl, her ex-boyfriend.

A real job. A paycheck. Security.

What a difference from her recent past. Skimming a few bucks here and there from deceitful unsuspecting corporations had been necessary. Selecting only the greediest and worst companies to steal from, she'd merely kept a portion of the proceeds to shelter and feed her family. The money had been used to keep Kimmie safe and away from Carl. The rest had gone to the corporations' former employees who had been laid off to ensure the bastards at the top got their big bonuses.

Now, she was getting real money, playing the role of a cyber criminal instead of actually being one. Her boss was a billionaire who had her testing his company's security systems. She'd already shown him that they weren't foolproof.

What a shock it had been to get Mr. Knight's introduction e-mail.

Of course, her first inclination had been that it was a trap.

She'd almost gotten caught last year when she'd siphoned ten thousand dollars from a known mobster. The FBI's trace on his transactions had captured her digital trail. That's when she'd left Kimmie with her mom and hit the road. It took three months of sweat and blood, but now she felt safe from being discovered.

God, she missed her daughter. Now that things had finally settled down, she believed it would be safe to go get her. With the big payday Knight was going to give her once this job was complete, she could have a fresh start with Kimmie and her mom.

When she'd verified that the origination of Knight's e-mail was TBK Tower in Destiny, her worries about it being a trap had subsided.

This morning Knight had e-mailed her a virus he wanted to test on the new firewalls. When she first tried it, no go. Then she put her tweaks in, and *voila*, she was in.

She was definitely doing her job. There had to be at least thirty or more sleeper viruses inside their network. The past few months had been more difficult due to the two new coders they'd brought on. The security measures were top of the line, but she'd broken each and every one of them.

The game with those two excited her.

She liked their handles. Tall Texan and Country Boy.

"Let's see what you do with the code I got past your firewall today." She imagined them as geeky-looking guys—oversized glasses, skinny, non-threatening. "Check. Your move."

This was fun for her.

Computers made sense. People never did.

Computers didn't betray you. People always did.

Computers were pure logic. People? Never.

Just two more weeks and her big payday would be here. *No more running.*

A bang shook her from her thoughts.

The front and back doors swung open at the same time, and three men with guns rushed in.

Her heart was racing. She stood and lifted her hands to the sky.

The one with hazel eyes looked at her with surprise. "I never expected you to be a woman."

The guy who had come in through the back shook his head. "Might be sexist, but me neither."

Her hands were shaking. "I never expected you to find me."

The one in the sunglasses kept his pistol pointed at her chest. "Name?"

"Jena. More importantly, who are you?"

"Gorgeous, we're asking the questions here, not you," the hazel-eyed stud said.

"You've got the guns. I know who is in charge." All she could think about was her daughter. She had to survive this for Kimmie. "Take what you want. It's all yours." Knight must've insured this place. He would be out nothing. Besides, none of it was worth her life. Kimmie needed her.

The handsome guy who'd entered alone from the back leaned

forward. "You working alone?"

"There's about five people that should be coming back from break any time," she lied, shaking her head.

"About five? Not true. You would know exactly how many people work here. Good try, miss, but cut the lies." The man in the sunglasses was quite attractive, too. But unlike his two buddies, he had a silver band around his wedding finger. He turned to the hazel-eyed guy. "Matt, cuff her. Sean and I will start carrying this equipment out."

What are they going to do with me? "Hold on. Are you the police? There's been a mix up apparently."

"You can say that again. On it, Dylan." Matt towered over her. Her five foot five inches didn't hold a candle to his six-two muscled frame. He wore a dark T-shirt and Levi's. Gold flecks sparkled in his hazel eyes. "Jena, turn around."

She complied, trying to think of a way out of this mess. Her mind was running several scenarios but none ended well for her. Right now, the best thing she could do was to cooperate until some better opportunity for escape presented itself.

Matt tightened the steel around her wrists. "While you guys get started, I'll call the Knights and let them know we've got Robin Hood."

Relief flooded through her. "You're from TBK?"

"Damn right. I'm Tall Texan," Matt told her. "Sean is Country Boy. You know us, don't you? Check mate."

"We almost had you back in Wyoming, Jena." Sean smiled. "You are good, but not as good as we are."

She sighed. "Congratulations. Mr. Knight is going to be very pleased you found me. You can take the cuffs off now. You won the game."

"Damn right we did," Sean said. He and Matt were similar in frame, though Sean was an inch taller and his eyes were dark. If this were any other circumstance, she would've been flirting with them. Once this got cleared up, who knew? Maybe she would go for it.

"I need to report to Scott Knight," she told them. "I'm an employee of TBK, too."

Dylan came up to her. "Don't even try, miss. We know who you are. You're Robin Hood. You're the one who has been making my job difficult."

"I'm serious. I've been working on a secret assignment for Mr. Knight. Call him. He'll clear all this up."

"Secret assignment?" Matt shook his head. "Get a load of this one. Quite the Mata Hari we have here." He leaned forward and cupped her chin. "Listen to me, Jena. You will tell us who you are working for or you will regret it."

"I told you already," she said, frustration building inside her. "I. Work. For. Scott. Knight."

* * * *

Sean grinned at the sexy auburn beauty. He'd faced dangerous enemies many times back in the CIA, but none more beautiful than Jena. "Our little hacker has fire, doesn't she?"

"Call Mr. Knight. He can clear this all up." Jena's green eyes and curved shape—an hourglass with a little more on top than on bottom—fit his idea of perfection. Just right. "I've got his Skype number on all the computers."

Like him, Dylan and Matt were curious about that revelation.

"You've been talking with Scott Knight?" Matt asked. "On Skype?"

She nodded. "Click on my contacts. His handle is TBK Prez1. He will validate everything I've told you."

Sean clicked on the "Video Call" button for TBK Prez1. Two rings and then the image of a face—not Scott Knight's—filled the screen.

"Fuck," Dylan said.

Instantly the screen went black.

"My God. Was that Lunceford?" Matt asked.

"Lunceford? No. Scott Knight, of course," Jena said.

"You've been duped, miss." Dylan typed furiously on the keyboards, trying to save the system from a total wipe. Sean and Matt jumped on a couple of terminals, trying to do the same.

"What do you mean that I've been duped?" Jena stared at the dark monitors. She was either the best damn actress he'd ever seen or she was as shocked as they were.

Dylan continued trying to bring the system back up. "That was Kip Lunceford, not Scott."

"Dead end here," Matt told them.

"Here, too," Sean added. The self-destruct sequence wiped out everything they could've used to get the viruses in TBK's network removed. *Fuck.*

"What do you mean that wasn't Scott Knight? What happened to my equipment?"

"I think you can remove the handcuffs, buddy." Sean told Matt. Then he leaned forward and placed his cell's screen in front of Jena. "Here's a picture of Scott."

Her eyes widened. "That can't be him. It just can't. I've been working for him for several months."

* * * *

"This sure explains a lot." Matt removed her cuffs.

Jena brought her hands to her front and began rubbing her wrists.

If he'd had any idea how gorgeous Robin Hood was, he would've worked even harder to find her, forgoing eating and sleeping.

Sean shook his head. "We have worked like dogs trying to get these attacks on TBK's system shut down."

"How can Kip Lunceford have a Skype account?" Sean asked.

"Hell, not just Skype. According to Jena, his calls came from inside TBK somehow. Any and all access should be impossible."

Matt sat back down at another terminal even though he doubted it would change a damn thing. "The creep is in a maximum security prison."

"You haven't seen his cell there. Thick Plexiglas. No visitors," Dylan said. "The only thing that's going to stop that fucker is a hole in the ground."

Sean sighed. "He had one visitor, don't you remember?"

Matt sure did. The Russian mobster.

"Guys, please clue me in," Jena pleaded. "You really are with TBK?"

He turned to her. The panic showing in her green eyes hit him in the gut. She was innocent in all this. "Yes. We work for Two Black Knights. This guy is head of security." He pointed at Dylan.

"Strange. Dylan Strange," his former CIA lead told Jena.

"And this is Sean MacCabe," Matt added, motioning to his friend. "I'm Matthew Dixon, but most people call me Matt."

"I know. He's Country Boy and you're Tall Texan. Who is this Kip guy?"

"Kip Lunceford worked for TBK a long time ago," Matt turned his chair around. "Have a seat, Jena. It's a long story."

She sighed and sat back in her chair.

Sean grabbed her hands. "Do you need a minute?"

She shook her head.

Matt knew Sean better than anyone. They were in sync about almost everything. It was clear to him that Sean liked what he saw in Jena. He felt exactly the same way.

"I'm sitting," she said. "I'm ready for the whole truth."

"Kip has been placing viruses inside the system for years," he told her. "You're just the latest person he's used to accomplish his goal of tearing down the company."

When he finished telling her the whole story about Kip, she looked down at her feet. "Damn, I was such a fool."

"Don't beat yourself up too much, Jena." Matt wanted to wrap his arm around the sweet woman, hoping to make her feel better. But he didn't. Even though she'd been a victim in all of this, he must keep his perspective. "Remember, he deceived everyone at TBK at one time."

"He's evil but he's also a genius," Sean added.

"You're no dummy, Robin Hood." Matt grinned, pointing to his chest. "Tall Texan knows. I've seen what kind of code you write."

"Should we bother taking this stuff now?" Sean asked.

"We better," Matt answered. "I doubt there's anything salvageable, but back in Destiny at TBK Tower we can make sure."

"I'm going to step out and call the Knights," Dylan said, heading for the door. "They need to know what's going on."

As the door closed behind him, Sean stood and began unplugging the equipment. "Let's load up and get out of here." He turned to Jena. "You're going with us."

Jena shook her head. "I can't go with you. I have things I have to do."

Did she think she was going to just waltz off after all the trouble she'd caused? She'd been working for a criminal for months. "You don't have any choice. We don't know what Kip or his associates want to do to you. Until we know you're safe, you're with us. Got it?"

"I can take care of myself," she said, unblinking.

"I'm sure you can, but Kip isn't just some hacker to trifle with. He's a serial killer." She was in way over her head and she didn't seem to realize it.

"But didn't you just say he's locked up?"

"Yes, but he's got connections on the outside," Sean told her. "He has Skype and no telling what else. Who knows how many associates are working with him."

"What kind of associates?" Jena asked.

"Mobsters," Matt told her. "One in particular we've been tracking by the name of Mitrofanov."

Her jaw dropped. "Niklaus Mitrofanov?"

Chapter Two

Jena couldn't believe her ears.

"How do you know Niklaus Mitrofanov?" Matt asked, his tone sharpening.

"I never met him," she confessed. How much more should she tell the sexy Texans?

"You're holding back, aren't you?" Sean asked. "What? Tell us everything. That's the only way we can protect you."

"Why should you protect me? You don't even know me." Life loved to serve her big piles of crap, and this had to be the biggest yet. A serial killer knew her name and what she looked like. She'd talked to him on Skype several times. Kip Lunceford, not Scott Knight. "I have things to do. Besides, I can take care of myself."

Sean leaned forward, ever so close. Her heart was racing in her chest. "What's more important than saving your life?"

Kimmie. She had planned on going to get her at the end of the month after the big payday. Neither was going to happen. She couldn't go to her. Not now. Not with Mitrofanov and Kip on her trail. Why not go with Matt and Sean? Because she had no clue what kind of men they were. Carl had seemed normal, too. He was even attractive, though not on the level the Texans were.

"I've got to get out of here," she said, panic setting in. She'd been running for so long. Would it ever end?

"You're not going anywhere without us," Matt told her firmly. "And we're not leaving until you tell us everything. Start by giving us your last name."

"White. Jena White." It was the last of a long series of aliases that's she'd used.

"That's a lie," Sean said. "That's not your real name, is it?"

How could he see through her so easily? "Yes, it is."

"You're going to learn to trust me, Jena." His dark eyes fixed on her. "Trust is hard for you I bet. Very hard."

Matt moved his chair next to hers. "Sean, she's been through a helluva lot today. Give her a break."

Today? The last three months of her life had been complete chaos. "This is my life and I don't have to do anything I don't want to."

"Well then, whether you know it or not, you want to," Sean told her.

Matt leaned close. "Jena, you need us. Sean is right about that. The more you tell us, the better we can help bring down these assholes."

She wanted to trust them with everything. Something inside told her they were good men. But she hadn't trusted her intuition on men since Carl. "I need to make a phone call first. To my sister." The last part was a lie. She wasn't about to tell them about Kimmie or her mom. Not yet.

"You can use my phone," Matt said, pulling out his cell. "Yours might have a tracker on it."

"Not possible." No way was she going to leave her mother's home number in his history. "I just got several burner phones this morning."

"You are definitely Robin Hood." Sean smiled. "No wonder we had so much trouble finding you."

"Go ahead and call your sister," Matt said.

"If you two will excuse me, I will."

"Can't leave you alone, Jena," he told her. "It's too dangerous."

They all stilled as they heard gunshots from outside the building.

"Get down," Sean ordered, pulling his pistol out.

She got under one of the desks and watched them both head to the doors, Sean to the back and Matt to the front. Dylan was still outside.

More shots.

They exited.

She was alone.

Trembling, she crawled to her purse, pulling out her gun and placing it next to her. Then she got the cell and dialed her mom.

Another shot. *Please let me live for Kimmie.*

"Hello?" her mother's voice came through.

"Mom, are you and Kimmie okay?" Her heart pounded hard in her chest.

"Yes, Jena. Everything's fine here. What's wrong?"

Thank God. "I just got worried about you, Mom," she lied, trying to keep her voice steady. "I've been away so long. I miss you and Kimmie. Just making sure you're okay."

"You want to talk to her? She's outside on the swing in the backyard, but I can go get her."

"Not now." She didn't want Kimmie or her mom hearing the commotion that was going on outside. "I'm expecting an important call. I'll check in at the normal time." *I've got to end this call.*

"Honey, are you sure everything is okay? You don't sound like yourself. Did you learn something about Carl?"

She wished it were that simple. "No, Mom. I'm just very tired. I need to get some rest. I love you."

"I love you, too, Jena."

As she clicked off the phone, there were three more shots. She picked up her gun and pointed it at the front door, keeping an eye on the back one as well.

* * * *

Sean ducked behind a Dumpster, his heart pumping like mad. Dylan and Matt were pinned down behind Jena's car. There were at least two shooters, obviously highly trained. "*Pozadi avtomobilya,*" one yelled to the other.

His Russian was rusty, but he knew that meant "behind the car."

These were Mitrofanov's men. Sean was able to translate more.

"Our orders are to hold them down until backup arrives," one of the Russians said.

He hadn't gotten sight of the fuckers yet. Dylan and Matt motioned to him to get Jena and they began firing, giving him cover.

Times like this, he didn't think. He became a machine. A tool. A weapon. His training took over.

He ran inside the warehouse and found Jena on the ground with a gun pointed at him.

"Jena, it's me. Come on. We've got to get out of here."

She nodded and ran to him. "Are Matt and Dylan okay?"

"Yes. You know how to shoot that thing?" There was no way he and Jena would make it to the van. They were going to have to take her car to escape.

"Yes," she whispered.

There were no shots firing. He wasn't sure why. It was quiet. Too quiet.

"Hurry," Matt yelled from outside. "We've got to get out of here now."

Hauling ass, he and Jena ran to her car as Matt and Dylan ran to the van.

Sean's pulse was pounding in his veins. "How well can you drive, Jena?"

"I'm an ace," she replied.

"Good, that makes me shotgun."

Pushing the accelerator to the floor, both vehicles raced out of the parking lot, squealing their tires on the pavement. Sean and Jena were in the lead.

"Up ahead," he yelled at Jena. "There are more of them waiting for us. They've blocked the road."

In the lead, she quickly swerved the car just in time to cut around the barricade, barely missing a tree. Impressed by her driving skills, he prayed Dylan could do the same with the van.

He fired his gun out the window, forcing the Russians to take cover, though some were able to shoot back.

Sean turned and saw that the van was right behind them. *Thank God.*

Mitrofanov's men raced to their car and began following them.

Jena hit the gas. The needle topped one hundred twenty miles per hour.

Reaching the main highway, he began scanning the road. "Look for an exit to throw the bastards off our backs. There's one." He pointed to the off-ramp. "Turn off the lights."

She did and made a quick right turn. He knew Dylan would do the same. A left, then another right. They lost them.

"Pull over, Jena," he said, looking out the back window.

Dylan followed and stopped the van just behind her car.

Waiting a minute to make certain the Russians weren't coming, he cautiously opened the door.

Matt ran to Jena's car door. "Are you okay?"

"I'm fine," she answered.

God, the woman was something else. Brave. Smart. And damn sexy.

"You're good, too, Sean?"

"Yes," he answered. "You guys?"

"We're good," Dylan said.

No one was hurt. It was a miracle.

The four of them inspected the vehicles, which had the only damage from the encounter. Bullet holes had penetrated the van and Jena's car.

"Damn, woman, where did you learn to drive like that?" Sean was quite impressed with her skills behind the wheel.

"My dad was a race car driver. He taught me everything from *A* to *Z* about handling a car. I also know more than most men about the mechanics. That's why my old Ford runs the way she does."

"Would we know of your dad?" asked Matt.

"Probably, but I would appreciate my privacy for the moment."

Sean noticed a change in her demeanor. *She still doesn't trust us.*

"Come on," said Matt. "We need to get her out of here and back to Destiny before they find us. We'll sort all this out there."

"Matt, you go with Sean. Get Jena to Destiny," Dylan stated flatly. "I'm going to engage local law enforcement to get the evidence at the warehouse back to TBK."

"Be safe, Dylan," Matt said. "Those Russians might still be lurking around."

"I will. Go."

"You got it." Sean put his arm around Jena and was thrilled when she didn't pull away. "Everything is going to be okay now."

Chapter Three

Jena sat in the passenger's seat of her trusty Ford with Matt in the backseat and Sean driving. Both men continually checked the road behind for anyone tailing them, Sean in the rearview mirror and Matt out the back window.

It had been many hours and there hadn't been a sign of anyone. The sun was coming up. They were safe now.

She was exhausted but unafraid. The bullets and the car chase had rattled her, but she'd faced much worse before.

I've been shot at in the past, but thankfully Carl didn't have good aim.

The violent storm of emotions back at the warehouse had passed. She was calm again. More herself. More in control. More than anything she was pissed—pissed that she'd been tricked, pissed that she wouldn't be getting the big check she so desperately needed, pissed that she'd helped criminals. A Russian mobster and a brilliant madman. They might come looking for her, but let them come. She was ready for them, and they would pay.

"You sure you're okay?" Matt asked for the hundredth time.

Men could be so thick sometimes. "I will tell you again, Mr. Dixon. I'm fine. Perfectly fine."

"Well then are you hungry?"

"If you will stop worrying about me, then yes, I could eat something."

"That's putting him in his place," Sean chimed in with a laugh.

"Really?" She couldn't help but grin. "You should talk. By the way you were holding onto me, I wasn't sure you knew I had ever learned to walk on my own. Believe me, I can. I've taken care of myself for a very long time. Bullets? I've been shot at. Being computer techs, I bet you two haven't before today."

"We've seen more action than you can imagine," Matt said. "There's a diner up ahead. If you're hungry, I'm starving."

"Now the truth comes out, Mr. Dixon. You're the one who is ready to stop and eat. Right?" Jena was enjoying their company. It had been so long since she'd flirted.

"How about calling me Matt? Besides, we need a bathroom break. I thought I'd mention getting a bite to eat to kill two birds."

"If those birds turn out to be fried chicken, then I'm game," she said with a laugh. The lightness of their conversation was making her feel better.

Matt smiled. "I'm actually thinking of a couple of eggs, biscuits and gravy, bacon, hash browns, and hot coffee."

"Stop it." Her stomach rumbled in response. "You've already won. We're going to eat."

"Matt loves to drive his point home, Jena." Sean turned off the road and into the lot of the diner. "You'll learn that about him in the next few days."

"How much longer before we get to TBK Tower?" She'd made no fuss about going with them because she wanted to clear things up with the real Scott Knight and get that bastard Mitrofanov and his sicko friend Kip. Until that happened, it wouldn't be safe for her to return to Kimmie and her mom. She didn't want to draw any attention their direction.

"We just crossed the state line into Colorado. Trinidad is the halfway mark. It's about five miles up the road."

"We're going to need to bed down somewhere. We've been driving all night." Sean pulled her Ford into a space right in front of the diner. "We can ask inside where a motel is."

"If you two cowboys are too tired, I can drive this girl anywhere. White Ghost and I have covered a ton of miles over the years."

"White Ghost?" Matt exited the back seat and then opened her door. "That's an interesting name for a car."

"Yes, it is." Jena had picked the name five years ago when she'd first gone on the run from Carl.

She, Matt, and Sean sat down in a booth and the waitress brought them three cups of coffee. After they placed their orders, Sean's cell buzzed.

"It's Dylan," he said. "Hey, buddy. You okay?" Sean held up his thumb, indicating his friend was safe. "You're kidding?"

Jena didn't like the sound of Sean's tone. Clearly something had happened after they'd left.

"We are in Trinidad. What about you?" Sean asked. "Got it. We'll see you back in Destiny. Be safe." He clicked off the phone.

"What's up?" Matt asked him.

Jena was dying to know, too.

"Dylan went back to the warehouse with the Odessa PD. When they got there, the place had been wiped clean. They didn't even find a dust bunny."

"That's why they didn't follow us." What kind of operation had she gotten herself mixed up in? "They must've been ordered to go back."

"You sure you're not CIA or FBI? ATF? Something," Matt said, smiling. "You've sure got the instinct for it."

"Why would you think that?" she asked. "I thought you guys worked for TBK."

"TBK is our latest gig, Jena," Sean answered. "We're former CIA."

Tall Texan and Country Boy were turning out to be much more than she'd imagined. They weren't geeks. They were sexy as hell and apparently specially trained in a whole lot more than coding.

"What can you tell us about the code you uploaded into TBK's system?" Matt asked.

"Scott Knight...I mean Kip Lunceford, sent it to me every

morning." She shook her head, remembering how she'd been tricked. "I made a few tweaks to get past the firewalls and security measures you two were putting in, but basically the majority of the code came from him."

"Robin Hood, you sure were tough to catch." Matt drank from his cup, his eyes never moving away from her.

Heat rolled up her body as she looked at the devastatingly gorgeous man.

"She's good with a gun and a helluva driver, too." Sean's smile made her tingle inside. "Quite the little package."

The waitress walked up and set down their plates, which were filled with delicious food. "More coffee?"

"Yes, please," she answered, and turned to the two sexy beasts. "I'll be driving White Ghost the rest of the way. No motel."

Matt's eyebrows shot up. "We just plan on sleeping, if that's what you're worried about, Jena."

"That's what you say now," she told him. "But I know good-looking guys like you are used to getting your own way. Always."

Sean laughed and turned to Matt. "She thinks we're good looking."

"I heard. She's quite the looker herself, don't you think?"

Sean nodded and sent her a wink. "She's got fire, that's for sure. Matches her beautiful hair."

"Even her green eyes sparkle with passion," Matt added.

Their synchronized gazes locked in on her, wicked and startling. Their eyes held hers, Matt's hazel with flecks of gold and Sean's a dark, smoky gray.

She had looked at them before of course, but now she decided to really take a thorough inspection of the duo. They both had dark hair. Matt's was a little longer and more ruffled. Sean's was closer cut and perfectly neat. Their faces, so unbelievably handsome, were chiseled. Nice, natural muscles, not the oversized steroid types. She could feel their power, their passion and possessiveness, washing over her, causing a secret shiver to run up and down her body.

Matt Dixon and Sean MacCabe had entered her life with guns drawn, but that wasn't the most dangerous thing about them—of that she was certain.

"Let's get one thing straight here, guys." She forced herself not to blink, hoping to give the impression of inner self-control. It was a lie. These two were mouthwatering yumminess, and she was imagining what it would be like to be with one of them. Which one? Didn't matter. Neither was a consolation to the other to her. "We should keep this professional. I'm here to help you find the bad guys as best I can. Nothing more. Got it?"

Sean grinned and lifted his cup to his lips, which were the most beautiful lips she'd ever seen on a man. "What makes you think we need the help of a girl from New York?"

She tensed. "Why do you think I'm from New York?"

"Accent is definitely New York. Long Island, right?"

"Are you some kind of mind reader?" Keeping her true identity secret had been necessary. Now, she had the strangest urge to tell them everything. She couldn't. No way.

"Not a mind reader. Just well trained." Matt jumped in, pushing his empty plate to the side. "But Sean has always had an ear for that kind of thing. He's also great at mimicking people's voices. Men's only, but it does come in handy from time to time. Or it did, I should say. Back at the Agency."

"Ah. That explains it." She turned to Sean. "You two have known each other a long time. I'm guessing since childhood, right?"

"Now who is the mind reader?" Sean smiled again, and she felt her shoulders relax. "Yes. We grew up in Texas."

"You look a little alike. Are you related? Cousins?"

"We get that sometimes, but no. There's no relation at all, though Matt and I are more brothers to each other than most." Sean sighed. "There's no one I trust more."

"We've been to hell and back, bro." Matt's tone matched Sean—

deep and heavy.

What had these two faced together, suffered together? Their sudden change from flirtatious to serious told her more than their words.

"Subject change." Sean's face lit up. "Let's talk about the here and now. You said we could use your help, Jena. I believe you're right." In a wonderful British accent, he said, "Miss Robin Hood, what say you we catch us some thieves?"

"You certainly are a wonderful mimic." Attempting a deep Southern accent, she answered, "My pleasure, Country Boy. My pleasure."

They all laughed.

"I'm horrible at imitation."

"You're not bad, Jena." Sean smiled. "A few lessons from me and you'll be able to fool everyone."

* * * *

Jena excused herself and went to the ladies' room. She pulled out the burner phone she'd brought with her. The others had been left at the warehouse. She would need to get some more, but until then, she would have to use this one.

"Jena, are you okay?"

The panic in her mother's voice crushed her. "I'm fine, Mom."

"Don't lie to me. I could hear it in your voice when you called hours ago. I haven't slept a wink worrying about you."

Her mom could be a bit dramatic, but right now, it was called for.

"I'm so sorry. I should've called you back but I fell asleep," she lied, not wanting to add more concern to her mother.

"Jena Anne Taylor, I know you. Something is going on." There was a pause. "Did Carl find you?"

Her gut tightened at the mention of Kimmie's father. "No. He has no clue where I am and more importantly where you and Kimmie are.

No one does."

"Thank God."

"Mom, can you put my baby on the phone, please?"

"You bet, honey." There was a long pause. She could hear her mother shuffling through the tiny rental house in Albuquerque, New Mexico, to get Kimmie. It was a two bedroom Jena had gotten for them. Very small, but all she could afford.

"Mommy, Grandma took me for ice cream yesterday. When are you coming to see me? I want you to take me next time. Please?"

Her heart was breaking. "Soon, sweetheart. Very soon. Mommy has some work to do and then I'll be home."

"You always work."

Another pang of guilt shot through her. "I will be there soon."

"For my birthday. You promised."

In one week. Seven days. "Yes, for your birthday. I can't believe you're going to be five years old, Kimmie."

"I'm a big girl, Mommy."

She was missing so much of her life. "Yes, you are. You take care of Grandma for me until I get there next week, okay?"

"I will. I promise. Will you bring me a present?"

She wiped a tear from her eye. "I promise."

"Bye, Mommy. I love you."

"I love you, too, baby." She clicked off the phone and renewed her vow to keep her daughter safe from *him*. Now, she had to make sure Kimmie was safe from Mitrofanov and Lunceford, too.

* * * *

Having the strongest urge to put his arm around Jena, Matt stood behind her in the garage in Idaho Springs, thirty-two miles west of Denver. Sean was next to him, watching her just as intently as he was. Jena and Floyd the mechanic were peering down into the engine. She clearly knew more about a combustion engine than the man did, or most men.

Her slightly bent position gave Sean and him an unobstructed view of her gorgeous ass. Too bad it was covered in denim at the moment. He'd been imagining her out of her clothes and under him since leaving Odessa, and he bet Sean had been, too.

They'd shared women before. Being in Destiny for the past few months had shown both of them that it could be more than just a passing fling, though neither of them was ready to settle down yet. Lots more wild oats to sow. Still, if they ever did decide to live the Destiny life, a woman like Jena would be exactly what he wanted.

Jena was like no other woman he'd ever known. She was tough, capable, and fucking hot as hell. When her White Ghost's engine had started missing back on the Interstate, she'd turned to him and Sean and smiled. Her green gaze had caused his balls to fill up and his cock to stretch.

"I'm thinking it's the fuel pump relay," she told the silver-haired man. "That should run five bucks or so. Let's try that first."

"You sure know cars, miss." Floyd straightened up. "I'll have to send my boy to Denver to get the part. I can't leave the shop and I don't have one on hand. If it is your fuel pump that needs replacing though, I'll have to send him back. It's an hour round trip."

Matt leaned forward. "Just get both. It'll save us time."

"Let me get my son on the phone."

Something about Floyd's tone told Matt that it might take more time for him to locate his boy than he was letting on. Likely the guy was having issues with his son. The mechanic seemed like a good man.

"Were you in the Corps?" Matt asked, looking at the Marine Corps flag on the wall.

"Yes, sir," Floyd said. "You and your buddy were, too, right?"

"Yes, sir. We were," Matt claimed proudly. That had been years ago, before the CIA, but he was still a Marine through and through.

Jena shook her head. "Let's go the inexpensive route first."

"Don't worry about the bill," Sean told her. "This is on TBK's dime. We need to get to Destiny as soon as possible."

"Listen to your boyfriend, miss. You've got just under two hundred thousand on this car of yours. The holes I spotted are from bullets, aren't they? Fresh, too."

"What if they are?" Matt asked, never caring to be interrogated by anyone. The guy was likely harmless, but one never knew.

"Sorry," Floyd said. "I can be too nosy for my own good sometimes. Besides the holes, this baby is in the best condition I've ever seen for a car of its age and mileage, but even so, it has the same fuel pump the factory put in. Everything wears out. Take a look at this old man." He pointed to his chest and smiled. Then he patted White Ghost. "I'll give you back your girl tomorrow and she'll be running like the showroom darlin' she is."

"Tomorrow?" She shook her head. "We need it today."

"Can't. Besides, all three of you look like you could use some sleep. My cousin has a motel just outside of town. I'll take you there myself."

"That'll be great," Matt said. He was tired and so were Jena and Sean. "A little rest would be nice. But we haven't had dinner yet. Any recommendations for that?"

Jena laughed and turned to Sean. "Does he always think about food?"

"Pretty much."

Matt didn't correct them, though looking at Jena had awakened a completely different kind of hunger inside him.

Chapter Four

Jena walked into the motel room with Matt and Sean behind her. There was just one motel in Idaho Springs. Since there was a big convention in Denver, just thirty miles away, every room in the tiny town was booked save this one. She was going to have to share it with Matt and Sean, and that was making her nervous despite their promise to sleep.

"We're lucky to get anything," Matt said. "It's nice, don't you think?

"I do," she answered. Thankfully, the room did come with two double beds and a sofa sleeper. She'd get her own bed and the guys would have their individual spaces, too.

"Jena, you can have the first shower," Sean said.

A shower would be nice, but she had a problem. "I don't have any clean clothes. I didn't see a laundry room. Did you two?"

"I didn't and I'm betting they don't have one, either," Sean answered. "I guess we'll have to wash our clothes in the sink."

"What am I going to wear in the mean time?" She looked around the room. "I'm pretty sure the Anchor Inn doesn't provide robes either."

Matt grabbed the cover off one of the beds. In a single fluid motion, he removed the top sheet and handed it to her. "Wrap yourself up in this, gorgeous."

"I guess it'll have to do. Are you sure it's okay for me to go first?"

"Absolutely," Sean answered.

"What about you guys?" she asked. "What are you going to do?"

"The towels will work for us," Matt told her.

"Okay, you got a deal." She headed to the bathroom, shut the door, and locked it.

She stripped out of her clothes and stepped into the shower. The warm water felt so good on her skin. She grabbed the little plastic bottle of shampoo with conditioner and washed her hair.

Thank goodness my hair has good body so I won't need to curl it.

"Why do I really care what I look like?" *Of course you care, Jena. Those two are sexy Texas men.* Her makeup was in her purse, which made her feel a little better.

Continuing to clean her body, she wondered what Matt and Sean were talking about. She could hear their voices but couldn't make out what they were saying. Were they talking about her?

There you go again, what difference does it make?

Be honest, Jena, you know you want them. Why not admit it?

The problem was, which one? She was attracted to both of them.

* * * *

Sitting on the edge of one of the beds, Sean kicked off his boots, and turned to Matt. "Jena is quite wonderful, don't you think?"

"I already know where you're going with this." Matt pulled out the sofa sleeper. "Either way, I have to agree with you, she definitely is wonderful. The way she handled herself back at the warehouse was something else, wasn't it?"

"So easy on the eyes, too." He would love to see what she looked like right now—all wet and out of her clothes.

Matt nodded. "Like you said before, she's quite the little package."

"We don't want to force her into anything, but there's nothing wrong with...strong hints."

"Let's just play this by ear and see where it goes."

Hoping for the best, he nodded. "Good plan."

* * * *

Jena hung her wet, clean clothes on the empty towel rack. It would take several hours for them to dry. She wrapped her body in the sheet, making sure it looked somewhat presentable and not like a white mumu. Her damp hair hung to her shoulders. She glanced at her reflection in the mirror again.

Makeup looks okay. Guess I'm ready.

She opened the door and looked at the two Texans in her motel room. "Next."

They didn't move or speak but only stared at her. It seemed like several minutes went by, but she knew it was only a handful of seconds at most.

"What's wrong?" she asked, glancing at herself. "Don't I look presentable?"

Sean stood. "You look absolutely beautiful."

"Gorgeous," Matt said, stepping up beside him. "I've never seen anyone make a sheet look so sexy in my life."

She felt a shiver go up and down her spine. *That's not because my hair is damp. I need to get ahold of myself.*

"Thank you. Who is going next?" she asked, trying to control her desires. "The shower is free. I left you two dry towels. Or you could fight over who gets the other sheet from the other bed. I wouldn't mind learning who would win that battle."

"Me first," Sean said in a tone that was filled with playfulness as he jumped up and ran for the bathroom door.

Matt raced behind him. "Not a chance."

She laughed. "You two could conserve water and take a shower together."

"We're not gay, Jena." Sean smiled and teased.

She gazed at them standing there, both holding onto the door. "Honestly, that didn't even cross my mind. I just thought you two looked cute running to the bathroom. You two always been so competitive?"

"Our whole lives," they answered in unison.

"Cavemen. I knew it," she laughed. "Let me help you out of this predicament." She grabbed her purse and pulled out a quarter. "Heads, Sean goes first. Tails, Matt."

Matt smiled. "Glad you called me tails, Robin Hood. I like that handle."

These two were trouble. "You're more devil than Tall Texan aren't you?"

He grinned wickedly.

She sent the coin into the air and it fell to the floor. "Heads. Sean, you're up."

He nodded and walked into the bathroom.

Matt turned to her. "Are you thirsty? I sure am. I spotted a soda machine by the office."

"Diet Coke, please."

He smiled and headed out the door.

Stretching out on the bed, she realized her willpower was shaky at best with these two. Besides, it had been a long time since she'd been with a man. In under a week she would be gone. Why not go for it? But the question still on the table was—which one? Her body sure didn't have a favorite. Neither did she. Tall Texan and Country Boy were sexy men.

* * * *

Jena finished the Diet Coke that Matt had brought her. They'd talked about things like the weather and sports, but nothing too serious—nothing important. Still, she felt so tingly inside.

The bathroom door opened and Sean stepped out in a towel that was too small and too thin for his frame. Her breath caught in her chest. The man's body was like a Greek god's, muscled from head to toe. His frame seemed to glisten in the neon light coming through the blinds of the motel room. Her shivers turned warm.

"Next," he announced.

"On it," Matt said, springing to his feet. He went to the nightstand and emptied out his pockets. Keys. Wallet. But what got her attention the most were the condoms and tube of lubricant. She hadn't expected him to be a virgin. But lube? *Are the women he's been with dry?* The thought made her giggle.

"What's so funny?" Sean asked.

"Nothing. Just feeling good right now."

Matt grinned. "I'll be in and out in fifteen minutes."

In and out? Another giggle, even though she knew he was talking about the shower.

"Make it ten, buddy." Sean's hot gaze remained on her. "I'll keep Jena company in the mean time."

As Matt entered the bathroom, Sean moved to her bed. He sat down on the edge of the mattress.

Ten minutes isn't long enough. She grinned at her thought.

"What are you grinning about?"

"Umm. This crazy situation."

He turned, placed her legs on his lap, and began massaging her feet.

"That feels amazing, Sean."

"Like we told you," he winked. "The Agency taught us a lot of skills."

"I wouldn't mind attending that class."

He moved from her feet and started rubbing her legs. God, his fingers were working out the tension just right.

After a short time, Matt came out of the bathroom. She couldn't believe it had been ten minutes, but her timekeeping skills around them seemed off-kilter.

Matt was dressed in the same attire as Sean, a single, tiny towel. His body was ripped. His hazel eyes were filled with heat. He walked over to her and got on the other side of the bed and immediately started to rub her shoulders.

"I guess Sean wasn't lying to me," she said, loving the feel of their fingers on her sore spots.

"What do you mean?" Matt asked.

"The training you guys got at the CIA. Apparently, the superspy Agency is putting out an army of massage therapists. Who knew?"

Sean leaned in and kissed her, devouring her mouth with his own. She felt his tongue trace her lips. Her toes curled and tingles vibrated in her core.

When he released her lips, Matt took his place, kissing her into a dizzy space of desire. Her lips throbbed from the onslaught of the two sexy men.

Which one should I choose? Isn't that what their kisses are asking me? "Come on, guys. Don't make me pick."

"What if we told you that you didn't have to pick?" Matt asked.

"I don't want to come between you two."

Sean brushed the hair out of her eyes. "But that's exactly where I want you. Between me and Matt."

"You read my mind," Matt chimed in, placing his hand on the back of her neck.

"You mean a threesome?"

"Yes," they answered in unison.

Sean kissed her again until her heart pounded in her chest like a jackhammer. "We want to share you, Jena. Tonight is all about you. Just relax and enjoy."

Matt stepped in and crushed his lips to hers. Her whole body was tingling from being passed back and forth from one man to the other. She'd never experienced anything like this, but her feelings were so strong she couldn't resist.

Sean leaned in and took her lips again. She melted into him as Matt kissed his way down her arm. They were making her feel so special, so beautiful, so…so warm.

Their hands wandered over her body. She felt Sean tug on the sheet until it fell off her upper half.

"Wow, your breasts are beautiful, Jena," Sean said.

Matt released her lips and leaned back, his eyes drifting down. "You're telling me." He tilted his hazel gaze back to her eyes. "You've got to be the most gorgeous woman I've ever seen in my life."

"You're just saying that," she said with a smile. "You two sure have the lines, don't you?"

"They're not lines, sweetheart," Matt told her. "You really are one in a million."

"And we found her in Odessa, of all places," Sean added. "Who would've thought such a sweet thing like Jena would've been there in the oil patch?"

Matt cupped her breasts, his hot hands causing a fresh bout of shivers to roll through her body. "Not me, but I'm sure glad we did find her."

Sean feathered his lips along her back. "Me, too, buddy. Me, too."

Every touch, caress, and kiss was raising the warmth and pressure inside her. She chewed on her lower lip, trying to ease her delicious suffering. Matt began sucking on her breasts and Sean continued kissing her skin. Her breaths halved until she was panting. She closed her eyes as every nerve ending seemed to fire inside her. Her nipples were taut and she sensed a line shoot down her body and to her clit, connecting the tiny bits of flesh into a circuit of want and need.

Sean tugged on the sheet again, removing it completely from her. Now she was completely naked, exposed to them in every way. They tossed their towels to the floor and she saw their cocks, which were both at least ten inches and so very thick.

Sean's kisses moved down her body until he positioned his hot lips just within a breath of her pussy.

"Please," she begged. "I need this."

"So do I, baby. So do I." His fingers threaded through her flesh, and she felt his mouth on her sex. His thumb pressed on her clit.

Matt's mouth was keeping her upper half on fire and Sean's was keeping her lower half molten. Quite the duo, and she loved every bit of their lovemaking.

"God, you taste so good." Sean's tone was lusty and possessive. "Give me all your cream, Jena. I want it."

Matt teethed her nipples, delivering little shocks of pleasure. Her body burned, every inch of it. Her need expanded and her pussy and clit ached.

They moved her onto her side, Sean continuing to lick her into a frenzied state. Matt left her breasts and moved down her back, his mouth finding a new spot on her to torment. Her ass. She felt his tongue bathe her backside and she groaned, sending her hands into Sean's hair. More shivers. More trembles. More everything. She was on fire as they licked on her pussy and ass.

"Come for me, Jena. Drown me with your sweetness." Sean's lusty talk was making her even wetter.

"Make us feel your orgasm, baby," Matt said. "Every single shiver."

Matt used his fingers to loosen her up back there.

Sean teethed her clit and sent his fingers past her swollen folds and into her pussy. The combination sent her over the edge and she came. The pressure released, washing through her like a warm wave.

Sean lapped up her moisture like a man dying of thirst.

Sensations soared through her as the climax rose, backed off, and rose again.

She clawed at Sean's shoulders, trying to hold on to anything that would keep her still. But she couldn't be still. Nothing inside her could be stilled. She was moving, thrashing, writhing between them, drunk on the ecstasy they were giving her.

"Yes. Yes. Yes." She panted over and over again. The release continued and she pounded her fists on the mattress. Never had she climaxed so strongly or completely. This was more than she'd ever felt with any man. Explosive and so intense. Now, she'd felt it with two. Together. In one bed. They had shared her. All that mattered was the heat of their mouths on her body.

Sean's lips grazed her pussy lightly. "We're going to make love to you, Jena, until you are fully sated and exhausted from pleasure."

"Pleasure? I'm reeling from what you've already done for me. I've never had such powerful sensations with oral sex. I can't imagine what it would be like with you two, but the truth is I want to experience more from both of you so very much."

"That's music to my ears, sweetheart." Matt massaged her bottom. "This is the most gorgeous ass I've ever seen. I can't wait to find out what it feels like to have my cock inside it."

"And I can't wait to feel your pussy tightening on my dick," Sean added lustily.

Are they doing this at the same time? How will that work? Still, their lurid talk was getting her hot and causing the pressure to grow again.

The guys put condoms on their cocks. Matt grabbed the lubricant and began applying it to her ass. Sean's thumb remained on her aching clit as his lips pressed into hers. She moaned into him.

Feeling both their hard cocks pressing against the outside of her body—Sean's on her thigh and Matt's on her ass—she wondered how she could take them both. *Is it even possible?*

She felt the head of Matt's dick pierce her ass gently. The sting lasted only for a brief second.

Sean kissed her as Matt drove in deeper inside her body, claiming her from behind. The pressure continued to build, driving her mad with desire. After he was completely inside her, stretching her beyond belief, Sean entered her pussy with his cock, filling her even more.

Yes. Yes. Yes. It's possible. It's incredible. It's overwhelming.

As they began thrusting into her body, her need hit new levels she'd never felt before. She could no longer think. All that was left was what she could feel—*in her body, on her skin, everywhere.*

Each plunge of their cocks inside her was taking her breath away.

She thrashed between them, her body wild and out of control. She wrapped her arms and legs around Sean and rocked back and forth between him and Matt. This was like nothing she'd ever experienced.

"Come for us, baby," Matt said from behind, the lust in his tone enflaming her craze even more.

She panted uncontrollably when Sean moved his fingers back to her clit, which released everything that had been building up in her body. A giant blast of sensations shot out of her like an explosion, consuming every fiber of her being. As her pussy began to spasm, she tightened her body, bearing down on their cocks.

"Fuck!" Matt yelled. "That's it. I'm coming."

"Me, too," Sean said, his eyes closed and his muscles tight.

They both thrust into her harder and deeper than before. Her breathing was ragged as she rode out the sparks shooting through her. She felt their dicks pulsing inside her body.

As her climax continued, more kisses and caresses came from the two amazing men she shared this bed with. She'd thought this would be a single night to remember. What she hadn't planned on was how strongly she would connect with them. Leaving them in a week would be hard now. Very hard.

Chapter Five

Jena put on her clothes, which were dry now. The guys were already dressed. She'd been the last to wake this morning. What a night. She'd never experienced anything like that before. Sex was something she'd enjoyed, but she had never known how mind blowing it could be until Matt and Sean. They were the most giving men she'd ever met in her life, in and out of the bedroom. No wonder her heart wanted more from them.

She looked at her reflection in the mirror. "You can't, Jena. You just can't." She got the burner phone out of her purse and dialed her mom.

"Hello?"

"It's Jena, Mom," she said quietly so the guys couldn't hear her on the other side of the door.

She talked with her mom for a few minutes and found out everything was good there. Kimmie was still asleep, so she didn't get to speak with her. Ending the conversation with the promise of coming to get them next week, Jena clicked off the phone.

She was so anxious to get back to Kimmie and her mom. The separation was killing her. She needed to help Matt and Sean bring down the Russian mobster and Lunceford as soon as possible. They were smart. They might be able to help her with the Carl situation. If they could, she would be back where she belonged for good—with her daughter.

Could she trust them with everything? She wasn't sure.

She put the cell back in her purse. Opening the door, she looked at Matt and Sean. "Any word from Floyd about my car? It would be nice if I could see it."

"No answer," Sean said. "Just keep getting his voicemail at the garage."

"It's a nice morning. Why don't we walk," Matt suggested. "When Floyd drove us here, it only took five minutes. By foot, it couldn't be more than fifteen minutes to the garage."

"Works for me," she said, ready to get back on the road.

The morning air was crisp as Jena walked between Matt and Sean.

Matt had been correct. The walk was short and pleasant. As they approached the garage, she saw her car sitting outside, freshly washed. It certainly seemed to her the work was done. Was it the fuel pump or the relay? She still was betting the latter.

They heard a gunshot inside the garage.

"Get down," Sean shouted.

She flattened herself to the pavement and pulled out her gun. Matt and Sean moved in front of her, acting as cover to whatever was going on inside. Like her, both men had drawn their weapons. They shuffled behind White Ghost. Another shot.

"Did they find us?" Her heart was racing like mad. "What about Floyd?"

Matt held his index finger to his lips. Motioning to Sean that he was going inside to check things out, he crouched down and moved to the left of her car.

"Go with him," she whispered, concerned for Matt's safety. "I'll be fine. I'll cover you."

Sean shook his head. "I'm staying. Matt knows what he's doing."

* * * *

Matt entered the garage from the back silently. The voices were coming from the front of the place. One he recognized as Floyd's. The others with the Russian accents he didn't, but he had no doubt they worked for Mitrofanov and had come looking for Jena. They must've seen her car from the road.

"I told you," Floyd said. "I don't know where they are or when they are coming back."

Matt's respect for the man was growing. Carefully, he moved forward and saw the whole scene. Four thugs stood over the old man and one of them had a gun to his head. The Russians had obviously gotten the drop on Floyd, but he'd wounded one of them. The handgun Matt had seen yesterday was being held by one of the bastards whose hand was bleeding. *Good for you, Floyd.*

The fire he could see in the old man's eyes told him he wasn't surrendering without a fight.

"You tell us where the bitch is who owns that car or you're dead," the guy with tats running up the side of his face said.

That's all I need to hear.

He grabbed a can of oil and tossed it to the other side of the garage.

It hit the floor with a bang.

The four killers turned and pointed their guns in the direction of the can. Their backs were to him now, just as he wanted.

"Hands up, motherfuckers. You're surrounded."

They didn't comply but whirled around.

In a flash, he took out three of them, their bodies crashing to the floor.

Before Matt could fire on the fourth man, he fell to the ground.

Behind the dead thug stood Floyd, holding a shotgun, which Matt had never seen. "Your girl okay?"

He nodded, moving to the front door to wave the all clear to Sean. "She's outside with my friend."

"Thanks, buddy," Floyd said. "I thought I was a goner for sure."

"I was happy to lend a hand to a fellow Marine."

"Much appreciated. It might not of looked like I had them on the ropes, but I did." Floyd winked. "I've got to call my brother. He's the sheriff and this is going to be the biggest thing he's had to cover in his entire career."

He saw Sean lead Jena into the garage.

"You're okay. Thank God." She wrapped her arms around him, and he felt his heart jump.

"Buster, this is Floyd. Get your butt down here. I got four dead commies on the floor of my garage. You need to come take care of it. I know it's crazy, but I'll help you sort it all out when you get here." Floyd ended the call and sat back down in the chair. "Do you folks mind telling me why these assholes were after you?"

Matt's CIA training told him to keep his mouth shut. Information was power. Always. He looked at Sean, knowing he wouldn't share either, despite how much they both liked Floyd.

"They were coming after me," Jena said, spilling the beans.

Floyd nodded. "Tell me everything, young lady."

She did, and neither he nor Sean stopped her. Training be damned, Floyd could be trusted. The guy had proven himself, taking out the fourth mobster.

"That's why we're headed to Destiny," Jena said. "Me and these two want to bring down the man behind all of this."

Floyd glared at the four bodies on the floor. "What a bunch of motherfuckers." His head snapped back up and he looked at Jena. "Sorry about my language, miss."

"A very good description in my opinion, Floyd."

"Smart girl. By the way, you were right. It wasn't the pump. It was the relay."

She put her arm around him and kissed him on the cheek. "Told you so."

They could hear a lone siren off in the distance. Floyd's brother, the sheriff, no doubt. This would be a delay for sure. They might have to stay in the motel again. Even though another night with Jena would be to his liking, Matt knew it was long past time to get back to TBK and to work on bringing Niklaus to justice.

We'll just have to wait and see what happens.

* * * *

Jena handed her ID to Floyd's brother, Sheriff Glass. He was collecting all their information for his file, but had already said it was a clear case of self-defense.

"Jena White, you're from Albuquerque, New Mexico." The sheriff handed the fake ID back. "My ex lives there. How long have you lived there?"

"Not long. Less than a year." She smiled, hoping he would change his line of questioning. Keeping her true identity safe was important.

"Buster, you've asked your questions. The doc has the bodies at the morgue. What else do you need from these good folks? They need to get back to Destiny and get to work on their case."

The sheriff nodded. "Let me call Jason Wolfe. He's the law in Destiny, and if he can verify your stories, I have no reason for asking you to stay in Idaho Springs. I have your numbers if I have any more questions for you."

* * * *

As they drove past the Destiny sign, the early afternoon sun above in the clear sky lit the landscape in a warm glow. Jena sat in the passenger's seat with Matt driving and Sean sat in the back.

"This place is beautiful," she told them.

"That's what we thought the first time we saw it, too." Matt drove them over the bridge.

According to the sign, the Silver Spoon Bridge was the only way into the town. Made sense since Destiny was on a peninsula. The lake around it was like a mirror, reflecting the blue sky.

"It's breathtaking." She sighed. The town was charming. Who would've thought it was home to two of the largest companies in the United States? Two Black Knights Enterprises and O'Leary Global had their headquarters in Destiny. Back in her former life, before the fake Scott Knight had approached her, Jena had never considered skimming from either company as their reputations were stellar. TBK and O'Leary were incredibly good to their employees and their customers.

They turned on West Street. The park at the center of Destiny was lovely. On each of its four corners was a dragon statue. As Matt made a right on South Street, she saw two buildings up ahead.

"Is one of those two big buildings TBK's headquarters?"

"The one on the right is TBK," Sean told her. "Our place is behind it only a block away on Second Street. We have the corner house and face the lake. You're going to love it."

When they drove in front of their home, she was impressed by its curb appeal. The yard was groomed to perfection.

"It's beautiful."

She walked inside and couldn't believe how neat and orderly everything was. The only clue that two single men lived here was the giant flat-screen television on the far wall.

"You hungry? We skipped lunch," Matt said.

"There goes your stomach again," she said with a laugh. "All I need is a snack or a piece of fruit."

"I think I'll fire up the skillet and make us some burgers."

"Now you're talking," Sean said. "I could use a beer. How about you two?"

"Absolutely," Matt answered, grabbing a pan from one of the cabinets.

"I would love one, Sean. Let me help you cook. Do you have lettuce, tomatoes, and onions?" she asked. "I like the works."

Sean opened the fridge and pulled out three beers. "Not only that, but we have cheese and bacon, too." He handed her one of the icy cold cans.

"You're singing my song, buddy." Matt turned on the burner and took one of the beers from Sean.

The three of them prepared the meal together, laughing.

She couldn't remember the last time she had so much fun making lunch. The aroma of the patties made her mouth water.

When they sat down to eat, she devoured half her food in a flash. "Matt, you should go on Food Network with your burgers. You could have a whole show."

"Wait a second," Sean said. "We helped him." Then he burst into laughter.

She and Matt joined in.

They'd been through so much together in the past couple of days it was good to have a light moment. Even if she'd had money to stay at a hotel, she was happier being with them instead. She felt safe.

"Let me help clear the dishes," she said. "I can take a bath after that and then we can go into TBK and get to work."

"Honey, we've got it," Sean said. "We've got three bathrooms here. You use the master. There's a garden tub in there with jets. I'm sure you would enjoy that."

"You're right about that. I would love a long soak."

"I have a shirt of mine you can wear while we wash your clothes." He grabbed her hand, making her warm inside. "Let me get it for you and show you where the tub is."

* * * *

Jena stepped out of the tub. The warm water had worked wonders on her tense muscles. How long had she been in the bathroom? She wasn't sure. At least an hour.

She put on Sean's T-shirt, which came to her knees. It was black with a Harley-Davidson logo on the front and an image of a motorcycle on the back, which made her wonder if he rode a bike.

She walked back into the bedroom to grab her dirty clothes, but they were gone, the space neat as a pin. They were the cleanest bachelors she'd ever seen in her life, and she'd seen quite a few single men at the track when her dad was still alive.

God, she missed her dad. Matt and Sean were the kind of men he would've definitely liked.

She opened the door and came back into the kitchen, finding Sean and Matt at the table, both naked from the waist up. They wore shorts and nothing else, giving her an eyeful of muscled man flesh to enjoy.

"We took our showers," Sean said.

"I see that." She saw that all the dishes were done and the place looked like it could've been on the cover of *House & Garden* magazine. "Where are my clothes? I need to wash them."

"I've already got them going. We'll head to TBK when they are done," Sean said.

"Let's go to the den," Matt said.

They all headed to the comfy sofa, and Jena sat between them. "I love your place, guys. It's so nice."

"Glad you like it," Sean said, placing his arm around her shoulder and pulling her in close. "It looks much better with you inside it." He leaned over and kissed her.

"That's not fair. I did all the damn cooking," Matt teased. "Give me those lips, baby." He crushed his mouth to hers, causing her to tingle inside. He pulled away and gave her a sexy smile. "The Food Network doesn't have any prize that's better than that kiss in my opinion."

Sean's gray eyes were dark with desire. "If that's the prize, I'm definitely game for learning more about cooking."

God, she would never tire of tasting these two guys' lips.

"First thing we're going to do tomorrow is go shopping for you," he said. "No more washing clothes every night."

"I've got an idea. Hold on," Matt said, pulling out his cell.

"What's your idea?" she asked.

"Don't, sweetheart," Sean said. "When the wheels are turning inside him, it's best to let his genius go on without interruption."

"Hey, Megan, it's Matt. I have a big favor to ask you. I have a beautiful lady with me in dire need of an outfit to go shopping in tomorrow."

"What are you doing?" Jena asked. *Who is Megan?*

Matt shook his head and continued talking to the woman on the other end of the call. "You're an absolute doll and a lifesaver to boot. Thanks. I owe you." He clicked off the phone and turned to Sean. "You know Megan, she said she'd bring several outfits by in the morning for Jena to choose from."

"Oh my God, Matt, that's asking too much of this woman." Taking a handout from a stranger wasn't something she was comfortable with. "I'll just wash out what I'm wearing tonight and put them on again tomorrow. They'll be fine. It's not necessary for your friend to bring me anything." *What kind of friend is she?*

"It is necessary, plus you'll get to meet our two bosses' fiancée."

"I would love to meet her, but—"

"No buts," he said firmly.

Then it hit her who Megan was. She knew Scott Knight was engaged, but the woman was someone else's fiancée as well? "Did you say our *two* bosses' fiancée?"

Sean grinned. "There's a lot to learn about Destiny."

As they continued talking, Sean and Matt clued her in on the town's quirky ways about all kinds of things, but the one that held her interest the most was how accepting the place was for people in poly marriages. More than accepting, according to Matt and Sean. It was the most common kind of family makeup in Destiny.

Matt and Sean had been so wonderful to her. Jena knew she was falling for them. Was it worth the risk to be honest with them? Opening up was something she so desperately wanted to do, but it also terrified her. "Guys, it's past time I leveled with you about my life."

"You're not obligated to tell us anything," Matt said.

"We are very happy with our little package just the way you are right now," agreed Sean.

"Please, I must tell you. It's important to me."

"Then go ahead, sweetheart," Sean said. "But nothing you can say will stop the way I feel about you."

"I know we just met, but we care about you, Jena. You must know that by now." Matt smiled and hugged her tenderly.

She took a deep breath, and for the first time in a very long time told the truth—*her truth.* "My real name is Jena Anne Taylor."

"Taylor?" Matt's jaw dropped. "Are you Bobby Taylor's kid?"

"Of course she is." Sean grabbed her hands. "You and I both saw how she drove back in Odessa."

"Yes, you're right." The painful memories burned fresh once again in her mind. "I'm Bobby Taylor's daughter."

Sean squeezed her hands. "Jena, I'm so sorry about your dad."

"Thank you." She looked at him and Matt and saw so much compassion. They were good men. Really good men. "My dad was the best."

"Sean and I were watching the race when that horrific accident happened."

"I'll never forget that day," she told them. Now that her dam of lies was broken, honesty flooded out of her. She needed to share everything with them. "I have a five-year-old daughter, Kimmie Marie, who means the world to me. I would do anything for her. I fell for the wrong man, if you could call him that. He's actually a bastard. He was my dad's pit boss. Everyone thought he was the greatest. He was terrific at his job, which helped my dad win many races."

Tears welled up in her eyes as she took a breath.

"Take your time, honey." Sean touched her cheek. "There's no hurry."

She had to continue telling them the whole truth about her life. "We were all so fooled by Carl Braxton. That's the scum's name. Dad had signed papers for him, putting Carl in charge of all of my family's finances. The bastard spent all the money or put it somewhere and Mom was left with nothing. We are still not sure how Carl accomplished that, but now it's all tied up in the courts. But the embezzling was only the tip of the iceberg. Everyone knew from the beginning that something was wrong with the car. Dad was the best race car driver in the history of that sport. So on that day, that horrible day—"

"Go on, sweetheart, we're here for you," Matt said.

"The investigation began. So many things were wrong, many things about the car. They realized someone had fixed the seat belt where it would not unlock."

Sean leaned forward. "That never came out in the media reports."

"The investigators kept things hush-hush, hoping to find the proof they needed to bring charges against Carl. None came."

"My God, I can't imagine how you dealt with that," Matt said.

"Dad couldn't get out when it burst into flames. God, just thinking about it is so hard. The investigators also discovered the lug nuts were loose on all the wheels."

Their faces darkened, clearly realizing the horror of her dad's murder.

"A slow leak was found in the brake line. It was an accident just waiting to happen. I'm sure Carl thought he'd covered all his tracks, but he hadn't. I had Kimmie two days after my father's death. I didn't trust Carl, so I kept her away from him. After I came home, I logged onto my father's old laptop. Getting past the passwords was easy for me. I figured out that Carl was robbing my family blind. I confronted him and he shot at me."

"Motherfucker," Matt cursed.

"I got away and went straight to the police, hiding Kimmie and my mom in a hotel that night. With today's technology, the detectives proved that the bastard had caused my father's death beyond a shadow of a doubt."

Sean nodded. "It's amazing how much easier it is to solve a crime these days."

"The monster was arrested immediately. It was also learned

during the inquiry that he was a bookie. Carl had fixed the odds so that dad losing the race would make him a millionaire."

Sean and Matt held her close.

"There's more," Jena said. "I was trying to figure out how I could support Mom and Kimmie. We had absolutely nothing. Carl had taken everything from us."

"How long before the court releases your family's money back to you and your mother?" Sean asked.

"It could be years. There's very little that has been found. Carl hid the money and we didn't have the funds to give a retainer for the kind of person it would take to track it down. I started trying to find dad's money myself. I found nothing but dead ends. I knew Carl had to be working with someone else, but I could never figure out whom."

"I wish we'd known you then, Jena," Matt said. "We could've helped you."

"Me too, Matt. The absolute worst happened. Carl escaped from jail only a few months later. He called and threatened to take Kimmie. He told me to watch over my shoulder, because he would kill me the first chance he got. He's been chasing me ever since."

Matt and Sean cursed under their breaths.

"I'd like to get my hands on that motherfucker," Sean said.

"Count me in on that mission, buddy," Matt agreed.

They want to protect me. She'd never felt like anyone had her back, until now.

"That's when Mom, Kimmie, and I started running. I was afraid. I know my mind wasn't clear at the time. I should've gone to the police. But Carl had escaped already. I wasn't sure they would be able to keep Kimmie and my mom safe."

Matt stroked her hair. "You survived, honey. Most wouldn't have."

"As our paltry funds dwindled, I had to find a new way to get cash. That's when I decided to become a hacker. It was so easy for me. Wrong, yes. Stupid, yes, but it quickly worked. I started finding corrupt businesses robbing their employees. I would take just enough to help the cheated workers and a little to take care of Mom and Kimmie." She closed her eyes, feeling the guilt well up inside her.

Sean kissed her on the cheek. "Your daughter is safe. Your mom is safe. You are safe. That's all because of how strong you are, Jena. You're amazing."

Matt squeezed her hands. "You did what you thought was best. Considering all you had to face, I think most would've done the same."

She looked at them. These two Texans had turned her world upside down. They made her want to be a better person. "So here I am, putting your lives in jeopardy, too."

"You're not putting us in any more danger than we were already in." Matt's gaze was warm and comforting. "We've been hunting down criminals for a very long time. That's just what we do."

"Can't you see that I'm also a criminal? I've just never been caught, until now." She took a deep breath again. "I have done things I'm ashamed of."

Sean touched her on the cheek. "You did what you had to do to protect your family. You have no idea how much that means to Matt and me. We'll deal with your past one step at a time."

Matt nodded. "It's clear we have several objectives we've got to accomplish. First, we need to get Mitrofanov behind bars. He's on your scent, and that's something we've got to change."

"I agree," Sean chimed in. "Second, we will find Carl and maybe we can have Niklaus and him share a cell."

"How?" she asked. "The jerk broke out four years ago and hasn't been found since."

"Honey, we weren't the ones looking for him," Matt said. "Sean and I have great contacts back at the Agency. Dylan has even more. The net we can spread can cover not just the United States, but also the entire planet. We'll get that fucker."

Knowing they would do that for her had her soaring and falling more for them.

"Third," Sean continued. "We need to get the malicious code in TBK taken care of. I think that will point back to Mitrofanov, so maybe it is part of our first objective."

"True." Matt's eyebrows shot up. "Fourth, we deal with your issues, Jena. We need specifics on what you did to survive. Every detail." He brushed the hair out of her eyes. "Sean and I have done some things in the line of duty that would curl your hair, Jena. Your duty is to Kimmie and your mom. We have friends who will be happy to wipe the slate clean for you."

"And we need to find your dad's money and get that back to you and your mom," Sean added.

"I don't know what to say." She kissed them both. Were they her saviors, her miracle workers? Could they do everything they promised for her? She bet they could and would. "No one has ever done anything like this for me. I swear I'll work my ass off to get that code out of TBK's system."

"Don't you dare do anything to this perfect ass," Matt said.

Sean cupped her chin. "You can work hard, but leave this"—his hand moved between her ass and the sofa cushion—"alone. Understand?"

Their commanding tones got her all tingly and warm. Carrying a few extra pounds around was how she saw herself. By the look in both their eyes, she could tell they thought she was just the right shape. She felt beautiful, and that was because of them. "Yes. I won't forget. Ass. Leave it alone."

"We, on the other hand, won't leave your ass alone," Sean said wickedly. "Let's strip our little hacker, buddy."

Matt nodded and stood, towering over her. "How would you like a little play, Jena?"

Play? "What do you mean? Role play?" That was something she'd never done, but with them she was willing to try just about anything.

"Yes, but specifically I'm thinking Dominance and submission."

"Like me being the virgin princess and you two being the sheiks who have purchased me from my father. That kind of thing?"

They both grinned.

"You're getting the idea," Matt said, stroking her hair. "Stand up for me, princess."

She giggled, deciding to play along. "Yes, Your Majesty."

Chapter Six

Matt gazed down on the most beautiful woman he'd ever seen in all his life.

Jena's fiery auburn hair and sparkling green eyes were captivating. She amazed him. She'd been through hell and survived. He and Sean had known a thing or two about that since they were five, the same age her daughter was. She'd given everything to her child. What a wonderful mother Jena was. He'd never had a parent that put him first. Neither had Sean.

He brushed the hair out of her eyes and took on the role she'd suggested. "Strip, slave princess."

Her eyes widened in mock surprise. "Yes, Sir."

Hearing a familiar submissive's address for a Dom from Jena's gorgeous lips was getting him hard. No, this wasn't hardcore BDSM, but it was good to see how she might respond to the lifestyle he and Sean had discovered years ago when they were still in the Corps.

Jena pulled Sean's T-shirt over her head slowly.

When it was off, she coyly placed it in front of her body, giving a provocative strip tease number. His heart thudded hard and his cock hardened fast.

"Does this please you?" she asked, continuing her role of princess.

Sean stepped forward. "Everything about you pleases us, honey."

"Our prize sure puts on a great show, don't you think?" he asked.

Sean nodded.

She winked, and his cock began to throb when she lowered the T-shirt to the floor, exposing all of her body. His eyes drank in every drop of the vision in front of him.

"Will you strip for me, Masters?"

Masters! She's a natural. Her round, luscious breasts beckoned to him to be touched, kissed, and sucked.

"You're not in charge here, princess," he told her in his most commanding tone. "We are."

She bowed and lowered her gaze. It might just be acting for her, but it was hitting primal buttons inside him.

"I've got an idea to make sure our princess is obedient to our standards." Sean stroked Jena's hair. "You'd like to prove yourself to us, wouldn't you?"

She nodded, her eyes wide.

Jena's zeal for sex thrilled him. She was fearless in and out of the bedroom. Feeding her every desire until she could barely walk would be worth it all.

"Princess, put your hands behind you and pull your shoulders back," Sean commanded her.

She complied instantly, which caused her breasts to push forward more. "Do you like what you see, Sirs?" She tilted her head slightly and smiled.

"Silence, slave," he said, taking the role more seriously. "Let me inspect the merchandise." Moving his hands over her breasts, he pinched her nipples slightly.

Her sweet little gasp got his hunger going. He wanted her. Wanted all of her.

"I promise to be obedient."

"Did you not understand me when I said silence?"

"I'm sorry, Your Majesty."

He wasn't really keen on the "Majesty" title. "Call me 'Master,' princess."

"Yes, Master."

"Ditto for me, pet," Sean chimed in. They'd shared women before. Their ability to synchronize their lovemaking skills to get women off was well proven. But Jena made him want to go beyond anything they'd ever done before. He wanted her fully satisfied to a point that she would never be able to forget them. Sean was a capable Dom, as was he. She would be completely spent tonight. They would make sure of that.

He looked into her emerald green eyes and saw her sweet trust. God, how could she trust anyone after all she'd been through, but there it was. Sure this was play. Sex play. Fun play. That took trust, too. He could imagine what it might be like with her at Phase Four. It would be life-changing. For her as well as for him and Sean.

He rolled her nipples between his thumbs and forefingers and felt them swell. "You like this, slave?"

She nodded. "Yes, Master. Very much."

He bent down and sucked on her nipple, continuing to pinch the other one.

Sean moved behind her and kissed her back. To Matt's surprise, he watched Sean retreat from them. *Where is he going?*

He could feel Jena tense. She'd felt his departure, too. *Damn it, Sean. What are you doing?*

"Where did he go?" she asked. "Is something wrong?"

He shook his head, but he wasn't sure. *This isn't like Sean.*

When his friend returned, he knew why and approved, too. Sean was carrying handcuffs, a box of condoms, and a bottle of lubricant.

"I think we should put these on our princess, Matt." Sean twirled the handcuffs on his finger. "Do you agree?"

She trembled slightly.

"Are you okay with that?" This was role play, and he needed to continue checking in with her.

She grinned, but her trembles didn't stop. She was excited and nervous, a wonderfully erotic mixture. "Yes, Master. Since it's handcuffs, maybe I should call you two police officers." She giggled. "I am yours."

I am yours. God, he loved hearing that. Was it true? Of course not. This was just play, amazing, over-the-top, explosive play...but still

only play. What would it take to make her his and Sean's? Much
more.

For the first time in his life, he wanted one woman. Just one. And
she was standing in front of him naked, exposed, and willing to be
tied up.

* * * *

Jena couldn't believe she was standing naked in front of Matt and
Sean. But she was. This was fun, too. Very fun. She'd never done role
play before, but had always thought it would be fun with the right
person. Turned out it was fun with the right persons, as in two guys.
Matt and Sean. They were opening her up to new possibilities, and
she loved every minute of it.

"This girl has been bad," Sean said, playing the cop role to
perfection. She liked the change in themes.

"I'm sorry, officers. Is there anything I can do for you to lighten
my sentence?" She looked at Matt, who had just pinched her nipples
again.

Sean put the handcuffs on her wrists in front of her body. "There
might be. Officer Matt, what do you think? Is there something this
criminal can do that will prove to us she's ready to turn over a new
leaf?"

"I'd like to turn her over my knee and spank that little ass of hers.
Maybe that will teach her a thing or two about how crime doesn't
pay." Matt's words shot into her. He was only playing, but her mind
was shifting to something more real.

She was guilty. The game was morphing between play and reality.
She needed to be punished for all she'd done. Sure, she'd skimmed
from evil corporations, but did that make it right? Yes, she'd sent
most of the money she got to the employees that had been laid off to
compensate the corporate overlords' bonuses. That still didn't change
the fact that it had made her a lawbreaker.

Sean kissed her shoulder. "Parking tickets are a serious offense, miss. Very serious."

"Don't forget, Sean. She took your shirt without thanking you properly."

"I didn't thank him."

Matt kissed her, making her lips throb. "Not properly. Bad girl."

"Please, Sir. I deserve to be punished." Would a spanking ease her guilt? Maybe or maybe not, but it would certainly feel good to have their hands on her naked flesh.

"Yes, you do, and I can't wait to see what your pretty ass looks like in pink." Matt sat back down on the sofa, pulling her over his lap face down, her restrained arms draping to the floor.

Suddenly, she felt a little shiver of nervousness roll through her that warmed up her insides.

"How many licks should I give her, Sean?"

"I want to spank her gorgeous ass, too. How about five each for a total of ten?"

Ten? Oh God, what have I gotten myself into?

"You got a deal," Matt answered him, and then turned to her. "Are you ready, pretty outlaw?" he asked gently.

She nodded.

His hand landed on her ass, delivering a sweet sting that sent sparks through her body. Another slap to her backside flesh hit her left cheek, and the heat rose. The next crashed into her right cheek, causing her pussy to clench and her clit to throb. Two more smacks came, one right after the other, slightly harder than the earlier ones, and she felt moisture begin to pool between her thighs.

"Look at this gorgeous ass." Matt's thick fingers caressed her bottom so gently. She could feel the heat he'd given her with his wicked slaps from the top of her head down to her curling toes.

"A work of art." Sean sat down on the sofa next to Matt. "She's been a very bad girl. I don't believe she's quite learned her lesson."

"You might be right about that." Matt shifted her over to Sean's lap. "Your turn to try to convince this princess to be a good girl."

Sean's breath escaped in a low, longing sigh. "My pleasure. Give me that sweet ass."

Now, she was straddling both of them in a prone position, though her pussy was grinding into Sean's lap. She could feel his cock through the denim of his jeans.

"One." Sean slapped her ass, sending a nice warm shock from where his hand landed all the way into her pussy.

She ground into him as the pressure inside her began to swell.

"Two." The delicious sting landed on a spot in the middle of her left cheek.

She'd never been spanked in her life, so the sensations rocking through her were surprising. She was on fire and loved every hot degree that rose inside her.

"Three."

Her ass burned and her head swam. She felt like she was in a trance, floating on the edge of a great expanse. Her need was so great it screamed for release, but none came. The pressure continued to build, but escape could not be found.

"Four."

She writhed on them, her hands held tight by Sean's wicked handcuffs. The role play had turned so very real. They were in charge. She was theirs to do with as they pleased. Nothing could be better. Nothing could be worse. Thirst and hunger were all she felt. Not for food or drink but for something deeper, something more primal, more basic. She wanted to be filled by them.

"Five."

The last slap from Sean's hand seemed to mingle all the hot spots on her bottom into one. The unification of warmth drove her to the brink of madness. Her need for orgasm robbed her of reason. The only thing that mattered now was to have them take her, completely, utterly—now.

"Please. Make love to me. I beg you."

* * * *

Sean stroked Jena's ass, loving the feel of warmth and softness it delivered to his fingers. "Have you learned your lesson?"

"Yes, Sir."

He took the bottle of lube and squirted out a generous portion on her ass. "I'm going to stretch you, sweetheart. Make you ready for my cock."

Matt stood and stripped. "I'm going to enjoy feeling your pussy tighten around my dick."

"Yes. Please. God. Yes."

He could tell that she was lost to her desire and couldn't hold back. His own lust was out of the gates and running. He wanted to fill her, to claim her, to possess her. Jena was like no other woman he'd ever known. Soft and strong. Sweet and spicy. Smart and sensual.

"We're going to fuck you, princess." Matt tugged on her hair. "You're ours."

Sean couldn't have said it any better. He removed her handcuffs and rubbed her wrists. "Feel good?"

She turned her head to his and he drank in her half-lidded, pleasure-filled eyes. "Yes. I feel wonderful. I want more though. Please."

Jena was so feminine, so adorable, so fucking sexy it was taking everything to keep his lust in check.

"We're going to give you more, baby. Much more." He wanted to get her hotter and crazed so that her release would take her to a level she'd never experienced. That meant taking his time to ramp her up even more.

Fingering her anus, he felt the thunder of desire in his entire body. His balls were heavy. His cock was throbbing. He'd fucked her pussy. Now, he would take her ass, an act of sheer dominance. She had the heart of a sub and that made his suffering grow. This wasn't going to be a second round of a one-night stand. What had happened in the motel in Idaho Springs had opened him up to dreaming of a new future—one with him and Matt sharing this amazing, wonderful woman.

Matt bent down, reached under Jena and began fingering her pussy, as Sean continued getting her ass ready for his dick. The moans that fell from her lips made him even harder.

Matt grinned. "She's soaked, Sean. My fingers are drenched with her juices."

"Please. I need you inside me." Her trembling lips sent a spark straight to his cock and balls.

Sean wanted her more than anything. Crushing need filled him to the max. Her pleasure, her desire to climax, her feminine shivers were all driving him wild and making him burn. He rose from the sofa, lifting her up into his arms.

As he walked to the bedroom, she wrapped her delicate hands around his neck and with her soft legs she squeezed his waist. God, he would love to hold her like this all night—her depending on him.

Matt followed behind and helped him lower her to the bed. "Sean, she's gorgeous. I can't wait to feel every inch of her again."

"Me either," he said, stripping out of his clothes.

Jena's face was flushed. Removing the last article of clothing, he gazed at her body and knew he was staring at perfection. Her curves were to die for.

He and Matt put on protection and crawled on opposite sides of her.

"Let's roll her over on her stomach so I can get inside this pretty ass first." He saw Jena tremble. "Then I'll roll her over so she's facing the ceiling and you can take her tight, wet pussy."

"Fuck yeah. That's a plan, bro."

"Please. I can't take it anymore. I need you."

"You've got it, baby." Now that she was facedown, Sean looked at her ass. It was a nice pink shade from the spanking he and Matt had given her. He rolled on top of her, positioning the head of his cock until it kissed her anus. "Take a deep breath for me."

When she did, he sent his shaft into her tight ass.

She groaned. "Yes. God. Yes."

In a single fluid movement, with his cock seated deep inside her, he pulled her with him as he rolled onto his back.

Matt got on top of her. They were squeezing her body between them, and for Sean it felt so right. His hunger hit the roof as he and Matt thrust into Jena.

She writhed between them, panting like crazy. "Oh God. Oh. Yes. Yes."

Feeling her body tighten around his cock drove him to the brink. There was no holding back his lust now, and he deepened the plunges of his cock into her ass. Matt did the same into her pussy.

Her screams of pleasure ignited the fuse inside him. "Coming. God. Yes."

As her climax took hold of her, Sean's body stiffened as he came, shooting his seed. His entire body was engaged. Never had sex had such meaning. Hell, it had never had meaning before Jena. Now, his possessive nature was in the driver's seat. He wanted her. Not just for now, but for always.

"Fuck. Yes. Fuck." Matt's plunges into her pussy culminated into a final giant thrust that rocked the entire bed.

They rolled her onto her side, keeping their cocks inside her pussy and ass. She trembled between them, and Sean knew nothing on earth could be sweeter.

He kissed the back of her hair and then he pulled out of her. He wasn't done. Not now. His lust was growing again. He took off the spent condom and rolled on another. Without hesitation, he sent his cock back into her ass, reasserting his claim of her. She tightened her body so that he could feel her body squeezing his cock.

"Again?" she asked sweetly.

"Fuck yes," Matt said, donning a fresh condom on his cock.

"We're going to make love to you until you think you can't take any more. But you will, baby." He sent his cock back into her pussy. "Much more."

Agreeing with his lifelong friend, Sean began thrusting into Jena again.

"Yes," she panted, thrilling him beyond measure. "Oh God."

She's ours.

Chapter Seven

Jena walked into the TBK Tower with Matt and Sean. The digital clock on the wall showed the time was 8:00 p.m. The parking lot had been nearly empty when they'd arrived. Not surprising, since it was past business hours.

The security guard behind the desk looked quite capable. "Mr. Dixon. Mr. MacCabe."

"How many times do we have to tell you to call us by our first names?" Matt led her up to the desk. "This is Miss Jena Taylor." He turned to her. "Terrence was active duty in the Marine Corps for twenty years. Sean and I only had four, but once a Marine always a Marine. It's a brotherhood that never dies."

"That's right, sir." Terrence held out a pen for her to take. "And what they didn't tell you is they were commissioned officers. I was not."

"Everyone knows that the enlisted men are the backbone of the Corps." Matt grinned. "Besides, you made it all the way to Sergeant Major, my man."

"You've got that right, Mr. Dixon, sir." Terrence turned to her and winked. The nameplate on his uniform showed his last name was McCoy. "I will never call them by their first names. It wouldn't be right."

The guy looked to be about her mother's age. He was handsome, too. Terrence seemed like a nice man. His eyes were a deep blue, like her dad's had been.

"Please, Mr. McCoy, call me Jena. I have no idea who Miss Taylor is."

"You've got a deal if you call me Terrence."

"Agreed." She signed the paper, and Sean wrote his name beside hers. "Terrence, is this all you need from me?"

"That's it, Jena. Mr. MacCabe has vouched for you." The man opened a drawer and brought out a temporary badge. He slid it into a slot that was attached to his computer, which she recognized as one of the latest models. Military grade. She knew that TBK had many contracts with the government, so it made sense to her.

Terrence pulled out the freshly coded badge. "You're all set. This will give you access to the building. Only the most classified areas are restricted to you."

"What?" Matt frowned. "We have the highest clearance. She should, too. She's going to be working with us."

"Not the highest, Mr. Dixon, but close. Mr. Strange and his wife, Erica, and the Knight brothers and their fiancée, Megan, have top clearance. You have the next best."

"We need to get that changed as soon as possible," Sean said with a laugh. "I've heard they have the best snacks in the Presidential Fortress of Solace."

She handed the pen back to Terrence. "That's quite the name."

"That isn't really what the top floor is called, Jena," Terrence said.

Matt put his arm around her. "It is by most who work at TBK."

"Not by me." Terrence turned to her. "If these two give you any trouble, all you have to do to reach me is dial 'one' on any intercom or handset in the building. I'm here until midnight."

"I'll remember that. Thank you."

"My pleasure, Jena."

Matt and Sean had their badges clipped to their belts. She attached hers to the collar of her shirt.

Sean took his badge and swiped it on the reader by the glass door that led into the main building.

There was a buzzing sound and Matt opened the door for her. "Welcome to TBK."

She stepped in, realizing this was the first time she'd been inside the headquarters of any corporation, though she'd been in several of the top conglomerates in the world electronically, including this one. What a difference to be present in the flesh.

She was impressed by the open space and elegance of this first area. The walls were several shades of white and looked more like paper than drywall. The way they twisted into one another looked more like a piece of art than something to divide one room from another. The workstations were immaculate, with the latest electronics available.

From this vantage point, TBK looked quite flush with money. When she'd investigated them as a possible target for her Robin Hood activities, all she found was how generous they were to their employees, to their community, and to charitable organizations. The profit margins were still impressive, but TBK was one of the few good corporations left in the world.

Matt and Sean led her to a bank of elevators, which also had a card reader.

"Let me try my badge," she said. "See if Sergeant Terrence set me up correctly."

"Knock yourself out, baby," Matt said. "He liked you. He might've made an exception and actually given you top-floor access."

She smiled, swiping her card in the reader.

The elevator keypad lit up. "What floor are we headed to?"

"Eight," Sean told her. "Not the top floor, but just under it."

She punched the button and the door opened. From a hidden speaker an electronic voice said, "Hello, Miss Taylor. Eighth floor."

She walked into the elevator and noticed the cameras. "The security here is very impressive." She knew topnotch safety systems, and TBK had the best. She was a hacker. Had been for several years. It felt odd being granted such access to the place.

"The projects being worked on are extremely sensitive. Some are for the government and some are for private corporations. Clearance and background checks are Dylan's responsibility. He's the head of all of TBK's security around the world, but here in Destiny, the level is at its highest."

"What's the keypad for?" she asked.

"That's for the executive level," Matt told her. "The people with access to that floor have to swipe their cards and enter a code to get to the fortress."

Sean put his arm around her. "There was a shooting up there before we were brought in several months ago. Security has gotten tighter."

"Eighth floor," the voice told them as the door opened.

"A shooting? Here?"

"Yep. Someone who was working with Lunceford," Matt stated.

Her gut tightened into a knot. The more she learned about Kip, the more she wanted to bring him down. Him and Mitrofanov.

They walked off the elevator and standing in front of them was Dylan, a woman, and another man.

"Welcome to TBK, Jena," Dylan said. "This is my brother Cameron and our wife, Erica."

To Jena's surprise, Erica hugged her. "It's about time they brought in a ringer to get those viruses out of our system. I know you can do it."

"She should," Dylan said. "She's the one who put them into the system."

"Dylan!" Erica looked at her husband, shaking her head like a parent whose child had just said something impolite. "Jena, ignore him. He already told me what happened. You're innocent."

"Robin Hood? Hardly." Dylan shrugged. "Though in the TBK case, she was tricked into doing what she did. I ran a thorough background check on you, Miss Taylor. I will be keeping an eye on you."

Jena tensed. *Does he know everything about me?*

"Dylan, that's enough." Erica stood in front of the man who was a foot and a half taller than her.

She saw a smile cross the man's face. Clearly, only one person could get Dylan to chill out and that was his wife.

"Forgive my husband," Erica said to her.

Cameron put his arm around the woman. "My brother can be a little too intense at times, Miss Taylor."

The three of them made a nice-looking...*triple? Threesome?* What was the right word for it? Destiny sure was different from anywhere she'd ever been before.

"What do you think of our workspace?" Matt asked her.

"This is all yours?"

"Ours and our team. We have about twenty-five techs who work for us."

This floor was a wide-open space filled with computer stations. On the walls were flat screens and smart boards.

"It's very impressive." She saw the top-of-the-line table computers, strictly hands on. No mouse. The latest in multi-touch technology. Secretly, she couldn't wait to get on those. "Very nice."

The setups of Mitrofanov and Lunceford had been good, but nothing like this. She felt like a kid in a candy store.

Kid? Kimmie? She felt her gut tighten. Her daughter would be turning five in six days. She had to leave here by Monday morning to make it the day before Kimmie's birthday. She looked at Matt and Sean. Leaving them was going to be hard. Really hard. But she must.

"Jena, now that you've seen the place, how about joining me and my guys for dinner at Blue's?" Erica asked.

"Thanks, I really appreciate the offer, but can we make it for another time?"

"I totally understand. You're anxious to get Kip Lunceford and Niklaus Mitrofanov. You don't know how much we appreciate you doing this." Erica hugged her again. "I am so glad you're here, Jena. All the ladies are already talking about the next shopping trip to Denver. You will come with us, won't you?"

"I think that would be wonderful," she said, but deep down she knew it would never be.

The Stranges went to the elevator, leaving her with Matt and Sean.

She turned to the two wonderful men and felt her heart begin to break. "Let's get started pulling Lunceford's weeds out of your system. Where do I sit?"

* * * *

With blurry eyes from all the decoding they'd done back at TBK for the past three hours, Matt finished off the sesame chicken. They'd bought take out from Phong's Wok, and Hiro and Melissa, the owners, had given them double portions of everything they ordered. He knew it was more for Jena, since she was the newest visitor to Destiny, but he got to enjoy most of the bounty since she'd only eaten half of her sweet and sour chicken.

He, Sean, and Jena sat on a blanket in the southwest part of the park at the foot of the Green Dragon statue.

"What time is it?" Jena asked.

He looked at his cell. "Eleven thirty."

"We should be getting back to TBK."

"No more work tonight," he stated firmly. "We can get started fresh tomorrow. Our team will be in, and we can give them some of the solutions you have designed."

"You've got to be the best coder I've ever seen," Sean said. "We've been on this for months, Jena. You've done ten times more on this tonight than we have in all that time."

Matt nodded, realizing how brilliant the sweet woman was. "I bet we can have Lunceford's crap gone in less than a month with your help."

"Okay, the compliments are nice, but I've seen your work, Tall Texan and Country Boy. Your IQs have to be in the stratosphere."

Matt smiled. "If ours are in the stratosphere, then yours must be way past the moon."

"The only reason it looks that way is that I was responsible for most of Kip's code being there in the first place."

Sean held up his hands. "Let's compromise, please, and agree we're all smart."

"Who said anything about you being smart, bro? Maybe a smartass." Matt laughed. He never tired of teasing his best friend. "I believe she was talking about me."

"Talking about you? Don't forget who rewired that Pac-Man game when we were thirteen."

"God, how can I? You never cease to remind me." He laughed, enjoying the brotherly banter with Sean.

"Hey." Cody Stone waved at them from the sidewalk. He and his two brothers were walking with their wife, Amber. They were all in club attire—Amber in fishnet stockings and daisy dukes and a half shirt, and the Stone brothers in Dom leathers. "Nice night."

"Yes, it is," he answered back. "Have fun."

"We will," Cody said, as the three brothers ushered their woman across West Street to Phase Four.

Jena said, "What kind of outfits were those? What's inside that building?"

Matt stroked her hair, gazing into her gorgeous green eyes. "It's the local club."

"Oh. A night club?"

"Not exactly," Sean chimed in. "Phase Four is a club, but it is a BDSM club."

Time to see if she's open to our kind of lifestyle. "Have you ever heard of that kind of club before, sweetheart?"

Her eyes widened. "A sex club? In this small town?"

"Destonians are very open-minded people," Sean said. "Yes, it's a sex club but it's more than that."

He and Sean always could finish each other's sentences. They had been in sync their whole lives. "BDSM is practiced by people who enjoy Dominance and submission play. It's especially great fun for people in love."

Jena's eyes remained on Phase Four's doors. She was intrigued and that thrilled him.

"It's about trust, sweetheart. Sean and I have been in the lifestyle for some time."

"Shortly after we got into the military," Sean said. "When Dylan asked us to come to Destiny, we were happy to see how accepting the whole town was to all kinds of people."

"It's sort of like the role playing we did this afternoon, sweetheart, only more intense." He reached for her hand and squeezed. "Much more."

"That was so fun," she admitted, which made him want her even more, if that was possible. "What happens in there?" She pointed to the club.

"We can show you some things privately at our house and see if you like it." His cock stood up and saluted at the idea.

"Yes." She giggled. "Please, Masters."

Hell yeah! He grinned and saw Sean was doing the same.

"Dinner is over." He stood. "Let's go home."

Chapter Eight

Jena stepped out of the bathroom wearing only her bra and panties, as Matt and Sean had instructed. Excited about what they had in store for her, she shivered when she saw them standing in their den waiting.

They both wore black leather pants and military boots. Matt had on a leather vest and Sean a black T-shirt. Both were mouthwatering goodness.

"Sit," Sean commanded, pointing to the metal chair in the middle of their den.

She was shocked to see what they'd done to the room. All the furniture was pushed back to one corner. She sat down in the folding chair, feeling the coolness of the metal on her ass through her silk panties. On the floor next to her feet was a white sheet filled with all kinds of sex toys. The dildos and paddles she recognized. The others, she didn't.

"Before we begin, Jena, we need to talk to you about protocols," Matt told her. "First things first. Safe words. The submissive—that's you—isn't without her own power. The sub can end any scene with a single word. BDSM is about pushing limits, but not going past them. Trust is the key. We will always honor your boundaries. The only requirement we have is for you to use your safe words. That lets us know how you're feeling with what we are doing to you. Understand?"

"Yes." She loved how serious Matt and Sean were taking this. They were being so patient with her.

"We're going to use some tried and true words." Sean put his hands gently on her bare shoulders, making her warm. "Like a traffic light. Red will mean stop. Green is go. Yellow is caution. Got it?"

"I do."

"Very good," Matt said. "Next, once we begin and until we end this lesson, you will address me and Sean as 'Sir' or 'Master.' Do you understand?"

"Yes, Master." She liked this play. Liked it very much.

"This is going to be a mini-lesson, Jena. Matt and I will be learning so much more about you tonight," Sean said. "All those toys you eyed a moment ago will likely remain where they are."

"Not quite all," Matt said with a wicked grin.

"Yes, Master," she said, getting into the spirit.

They both laughed.

"Our girl is going to be trouble," Sean said. "We might use a few things tonight, but this lesson is going to be pretty vanilla."

"I like vanilla, but what are the other flavors, Sir?"

"Trouble with a capital *T*." Matt bent down and pinched both of her nipples through her bra.

The sting shocked her, but the sensation it delivered quickly had her squirming on the chair.

"What color are you right now, sub?" Matt asked firmly.

"Green, Master," she confessed, feeling warmth wash over her. "Green is my favorite color. Have I ever told you that before? I want more green, Sirs."

"We have our hands full with this one, Matt," Sean said, smiling.

"You're telling me." Matt stroked her hair. "She's so freaking eager."

"True, but she's got to know who's in charge." Sean tugged on her hair, forcing her head to tilt back a bit.

She gazed into his eyes, which were tugging on her heart.

"That's better, baby." He removed her bra and tossed it to the side.

Her nipples tightened as he cupped her breasts.

"Stand up." Sean's commanding tone made her tremble.

She obeyed. "Like this, Sir?"

He and Matt smiled.

Matt stepped forward and Sean grabbed one of the vibrators.

"Color?" Matt's fingers curled around the top of her panties.

"Green, Master." *So freaking green!*

As he pulled her silk thong down to her ankles, she heard the hum of the vibrator in Sean's hand.

"Put your hands behind your back and clasp your fingers together," Sean ordered. "You keep them there until Matt or I say you can unclasp them, understand?"

Liking the dominance they both were showing her, she nodded.

As she locked her hands together behind her back, a shiver ran up and down her spine.

"Very good, sub," Matt said.

Sean held the toy in front of her face. The humming sound called to her need.

"Let me remind you, baby, one more time," he said. "You will keep your hands behind your back no matter what. Am I clear?"

"Yes, Sir. I understand."

He smiled and traced the tip of the toy down her arm, causing her to shiver.

Matt moved behind her, taking a seat in the chair. When he licked her ass, she began to squirm.

"Hands together until we say you can release them." Sean knelt down in front of her, dragging the vibrator down.

When it fluttered on her pussy, she became instantly wet. Though she didn't want to keep her hands clasped, she tightened her fingers together to obey his command. The pressure was so overwhelming, she wanted to reach out and grab Sean. She knew she had to control herself, although her body was telling her differently.

This is so hard, but the pleasure is wonderful.

Matt continued to lick her backside as Sean used the toy on her front, grazing her clit just right.

She closed her eyes and chewed on her lower lip, forcing herself to continue following the one instruction she'd be given. Hands behind her back. But the more they fondled her, the more heat rolled through her body. As her control began to slip away, she felt her fingers begin to loosen.

"Stop, Sean," Matt called out, stopping his oral assault on her ass. "She's about to unclasp her hands."

Sean removed the toy.

Instantly, she missed the feeling of the vibrator and Matt's tongue on her. "Please, Sirs," she said, tightening her fingers back together. "I'm sorry."

Sean's face was stern. She wanted to please him and Matt more than anything right now.

"What color state are you in, sub?" Sean asked.

"Green, Sir."

He nodded his approval and brought the vibrator back to her pussy, right where it belonged. She felt Matt renew his efforts on her ass.

No way would she unclasp her hands. Never. Not until they told her she could. She wanted to feel the crazy trembles their touches were inciting in her body.

Sean removed the toy, replacing it with his wicked mouth. Feeling his and Matt's tongues on her flesh sent an undulation through her body.

"I want to taste your sweet juices, sub," Sean said. "You've done very well. Time for your reward. Free your hands and come for us."

"Oh yes," she said, releasing her fingers and bringing them to his shoulders.

When Matt sent a finger into her ass and Sean teethed her clit, the hot pressure inside her exploded into a million sensations, all hot, all electric, all wet.

She cried out, raking her nails into Sean's skin. Her body tensed, feeling the overpowering orgasm coming to a peak, and then it completely relaxed. She was totally sated.

They'd showed her a new way of being, a way she wanted to experience again and again. This life was for her.

This was pure bliss.

Chapter Nine

The next morning Jena woke up due to setting her faithful alarm in her head the night before. It had never failed her. All she had to do was say she wanted to wake up at whatever time and she would. It required no wires or batteries, just her dependable brain.

I have to get out of bed without waking Matt and Sean.

Getting up between the two gorgeous men would be quite a feat though. She had never seen such a large bed in her life. Much larger than a king size. It had to be custom made, but they still had slept very close to her.

The sex had been amazing again, and again and again.

Mmm. Okay, Jena, get back on track.

Slowly, very slowly. *Voila.* She grabbed Sean's shirt and proceeded to the bathroom. Her ultimate goal was to show them she was no slouch in the kitchen. She started looking for a toothbrush and of course there was a brand-new one still in its package, along with a new tube of toothpaste. Did they always think of everything? The bedroom they were in was for guests. She wondered whom else they had entertained there.

What a ridiculous thought, Jena. You know you have to leave in a few days. But oh, if I could stay and bring Kimmie and Mom. What a wonderful dream, but you have to face it, it is only a dream. I need to keep my heart in check, but damn, is it already too late? They are the most wonderful men I have ever met in my entire life. Ever. Even if it could work, would Mom ever understand this lifestyle? Oh, for God's sake, Jena, get to the kitchen and see what these Texans have on hand.

She cooked sausage, bacon, eggs, and Belgian waffles. She poured orange juice and made a pot of coffee.

After setting the table, she saw Matt and Sean emerge from the bedroom wearing only underwear. That suited her just fine.

"I thought I smelled something cooking." Matt put his arm around her. "You did all this?"

"Me and the elves, but they belonged to the union and had to leave."

Sean came over and kissed her. "Thank you, baby."

"You're welcome. Sit. Let's eat."

"Damn, woman, you're quite the package," Sean said after eating his last bite.

"I believe I've heard that before, but thank you. Now, guys, if you'll excuse me, I would at least like to get some makeup on and dress before Mrs. Knight arrives. I believe you two can handle cleanup."

"God, you're a feisty dame." Matt laughed.

"That she is," replied Sean.

* * * *

After they were all cleaned up and dressed, Jena looked out the window and saw a red Corvette convertible enter the driveway.

A beautiful blonde, carrying several packages, stepped out of the car.

"Just look at her. She is absolutely stunning." She turned to Matt and Sean. "Let me ask you guys something. Do you have to be beautiful or handsome to be a resident of this town?"

"No, of course not," Matt answered. "But if it were a requirement, you'd have no trouble whatsoever."

"We have all types like any other town—short, fat, tall, slim. But no matter what they look like, Destiny has the nicest, most caring people in the world," Sean said, smiling.

"If only…" *But I have to leave. There's no way I can stay.*

"If only what, darlin?" Matt asked.

She wasn't ready to answer him. "Come on, guys, let's go help your bosses' fiancée."

They walked out of the house.

"Hello," Megan said. She was younger than Jena had thought she would be. They had to be almost the same age.

"Hey, Megan," Sean said, scooping up the two packages she was carrying.

"There's more in the car," the woman told him.

"I'll get them." Matt pulled out several outfits on hangers.

"And you must be Jena." Mrs. Knight walked up to her and gave her a hug just like Erica, Dylan's wife, had. Seemed like everyone from this town liked to hug strangers.

"Mrs. Knight, this is too much. I could've worn what I have on to shop for clothes. The guys shouldn't have asked you to do this."

"First, please call me Megan. Second, this is my pleasure. Why don't we go inside and see if these clothes fit you? We look to be about the same size, so I'm betting they will. What size shoe do you wear?"

"Seven."

"Same as me. Perfect."

They headed into Matt and Sean's house. The guys were loaded down with Megan's offerings.

"Where's the best place to try these on?" Megan asked.

"Back there." Matt pointed to the bedroom where Jena had spent the night with him and Sean. "It's got a full-length mirror."

"Excellent. You two cowboys stay out here," Megan told them.

Jena thought she was so down to earth. Except for the designer clothes she wore, it was hard to believe she was engaged to billionaires.

The guys piled the clothes on the bed and left her and Megan alone.

When the door closed, she turned to the gift giver. "Really, I can't thank you enough, but I only need one outfit. You have at least seven here."

"Actually, thirteen, but who's counting?" Megan sat on the bed. "Let's see what you look like in this red dress."

"I see arguing with you is a losing battle." She liked the woman very much.

"You're right about that, Jena." Megan smiled. "My two fiancés have spoiled me rotten. I'm on my third closet already. I will never miss any of these."

"Wow. You must feel like a princess." Jena slipped into the red dress and saw the tag dangling from it. "This is brand new."

"See. I have at least five red dresses already. God, you look gorgeous in it. The fit looks perfect. How does it feel?"

She turned to the full-length mirror and gasped. Never had she worn such a lovely thing in her life. Growing up, she'd been more of a tomboy, comfortable in jeans and a shirt in her dad's garage. She'd had gowns before that her dad bought her for the dances and proms at school. Even in college, he'd set her up with quite a wardrobe. Her family had been well off back then, but nothing like Megan and her men were. Daring another glance at the tag, her jaw dropped.

"I see that look in your eyes," Megan said. "I've had it myself before. Give a girl a break and take these clothes off my hands. It would take me a year to go through all the new stuff Scott and Eric have bought me if I only wore them one time each. I can't blame them. I actually do love shopping myself."

"It's been ages since I went shopping," she confessed.

"This is a beautiful town but I promise you can't get everything you need here, Jena."

"It doesn't look like I need anything if I agree to keep the treasures you've brought me today." She slipped on some heels, which were from another top designer.

"You are keeping them. I'm putting my foot down about that. Try this green blouse on. It will make your eyes pop." Megan handed her the top. "Besides, it would be fun to have you go with some of my friends on our monthly shopping spree in Denver."

Megan's sunny demeanor was infectious. Jena had never had a girlfriend before, but Megan was the kind of woman who would be perfect for that role. What were her friends like? *But I'm leaving in a few days. My kind of life doesn't allow me to have friends.*

"That looks great on you, Jena. Perfect for shopping." Megan smiled. "Let's get your guys' opinions on this."

Your guys? She didn't correct Megan, enjoying the fantasy of the moment.

Standing in front of Matt and Sean, she twirled around. "So? What do you think?"

"You're the most beautiful woman we've ever seen in our life," Sean said. "No offense, Megan."

"None taken. I totally understand. I've seen that look in my own two cowboys' eyes." Megan turned to her. "Time for you and me to go shopping, Jena."

"Hold on," Matt said. "We're going, too."

"I'm not sure you guys would enjoy the kind of shopping I've got planned today for Jena."

"Doesn't matter," Sean said. "You remember what happened with you. Well, it looks like Kip is back."

Megan nodded. "Yeah. Scott and Eric told me about what you saw at the warehouse in Odessa. My damn ex is such a bastard."

Jena was shocked. That sweet woman had been married to a criminal? "Kip Lunceford is your ex-husband?"

"Let's go shopping and I'll tell you all about it at lunch."

Jena wasn't sure what she was going to do. Her current finances would only allow her to buy underwear.

Matt and Sean's stares made her squirm.

"Honey, we've got this," Matt said.

Sean nodded. "We're the reason you didn't have time to pack

your clothes because we hit the road so fast."

Somehow they'd seen it on her face that she was worried about money. God, keeping secrets from them might be impossible for her.

"Nonsense." Megan put her hands on her hips. "This is on TBK's tab. Eric and Scott are putting her on the payroll. Jena is getting a clothing allowance."

"What? I don't understand," she said. *I must leave in less than a week.* "I'm only going to help these two get the code that I was uploading into TBK's system removed. Hopefully, that will lead the authorities to get something on Mitrofanov and your ex."

Megan came up and put her arm around her. "You're getting a paycheck, Jena. That's final. Shall I show you and these two bundles of testosterone the best shopping Destiny has to offer?"

"I suppose so," she said with a grin. If the other citizens were anything like Megan, this was going to be quite the shopping trip.

* * * *

Matt stood inside the boutique by the entrance. Megan had led them to the middle of West Street on the town square to Riley's Body Decorations, a combination dress shop and tattoo parlor.

Sean had gone to find Dylan, who had left a message that he had new information.

Jena was smiling from ear to ear. "What about this one?"

She wore a pale blue dress that emphasized her cute figure.

"You look wonderful, sweetheart."

Every outfit she modeled for him looked great on her. What wouldn't? Hell, a gunnysack would shine on her body. He actually liked her out of clothes more than in them, so he wasn't sure why she kept asking his opinion. It would always be the same.

"I think you should try on that mini skirt," Megan said. "I bet that would get a big reaction from him."

"You might be right. We'll be back shortly."

"I'll be waiting."

As they trotted off, he grinned. The only things that had really caught his attention were a pair of knee-high leather boots she'd worn for him. He could imagine her wearing them and nothing else. Of course, the image of Jena most prominent in his thoughts was with her under him. Her long, beautiful legs covered in the boots would be slung around his waist.

Keep alert, Agent MacCabe. You've got a job to do.

He kept his hand on the butt of his gun, which was under his jacket. He didn't expect Mitrofanov or Lunceford to show, but if either of them did—or their cohorts—he'd be ready.

The door opened, and he tensed for a moment and then relaxed, seeing the four men who came in.

Sean led the way, followed by Dylan, Sheriff Jason, and the two Knight brothers.

"Where's our girl?" Eric asked.

"In the dressing room with Jena," he told them. "They should be out to model another outfit any minute."

"Robin Hood. I can't wait to meet her," Scott said. "She's a very talented coder."

"That's quite the understatement," Dylan chimed in. "Kip selected her because she is brilliant. She was only a few months away from graduating with her Master's from MIT. According to some of her professors I was able to talk to, she was one of their very best. They were shocked when she fell off the map."

Matt recalled Jena telling them about her past. His gut coiled into a knot. Wherever her ex was, he better not show his face in Destiny. "She's Bobby Taylor's kid. You know, the race car driver who got killed in a crash about five years ago."

"That's news to me," Jason said, turning to Dylan. "I'm listening. We all are. Give us the details on what you've learned since the incident in Odessa."

"As you all know, the warehouse was cleaned out when I got back there with the local authorities. I made several inquiries to some friends in the Agency and found out that the only visit Kip has ever had from Mitrofanov is the one we already know about."

"Are you saying they're not working together?" Sean asked.

"I'm not saying one way or the other. I'll let the facts speak for themselves. Mitrofanov only went to Kip's cell once, but a couple of his men went several times after that."

"I thought the warden was a tough case and had locked Lunceford up tighter than a drum," Scott said.

Dylan nodded. "The warden is a straight shooter by all accounts I could find. Kip is classified as maximum custody. His cell is equipped with a toilet, sink, bed, and mattress. He has no contact with any other inmate. Out-of-cell time is limited to outdoor exercise in a secured area two hours a day, three times a week, and a shower three times a week. Correction officers deliver his meals at the cell's front. Personal property is limited to hygiene items, two books, and writing materials. He is not allowed any electronics. He gets no phone calls but is allowed, by law, limited non-contact visitations once a week. Kip has had at least one visitor every week for many months."

"Mitrofanov's men." Matt admired Dylan's unearthing of the information. The guy had always been good at getting to the core of an investigation or mission in no time flat.

"I still need to check around to verify it was Mitrofanov's thugs, but all indications point to that being the case." Dylan looked at his cell. "It's a text from Erica. As usual, the ladies are getting the Destiny Welcome Wagon out for Jena."

"Megan's rallied the troops for a party for Ms. Robin Hood tonight," Scott said.

"At our house," Eric added.

Matt smiled. The people of Destiny were so very kind.

The door to the boutique opened. He swung around, ready to draw his gun should he need to. Sean's hand was inside his jacket as well.

The person who walked in shocked him. Shane Blue, Phoebe's

brother, a recent parolee.

"What are you doing here?" Jason snapped.

Shane's eyes widened. "I didn't expect to see you, Sheriff. I came to talk to Dylan."

"I asked my cousin to come." Dylan seemed a little surprised by Shane's sudden appearance. Odd. That wasn't like Dylan. "We can use him on this." He returned to his normal stoic demeanor.

"Use him?" The sheriff spun around and faced Dylan. "He's a convicted felon. What the hell can he do for us on this investigation?"

"Damn, Jason. Think. Shane's been to prison, and, in fact, he was in the same prison as Kip is now. Shane knows the ins and outs."

Matt knew Dylan well and respected him. It was clear to him that Dylan and the convict respected one another.

"What can you tell us about Mitrofanov and Lunceford's connection to each other?" Sean asked.

"Nothing yet, but I'll check with some cellmates Tuesday when they can take calls," Shane told them. "They're not in maximum like Kip, but they know that entire prison, including his block, like the back of their hands. Nothing goes down that they're not aware of."

"From drug dealer to prison squealer," Jason mocked. "I wouldn't believe a word that comes out of your mouth."

"I know," Shane said calmly. "I'll tell you what I learn and you guys do with it what you want. I don't want the Russian mobsters here anymore than you do. This is my hometown, too." Without waiting, the man turned and left the boutique.

"I'm going to keep an eye on that one," the sheriff said.

"Don't let the past taint your opinion on my cousin," Dylan said. "He served his time. He deserves a second chance."

"I've been appointed as Shane's probation officer. It's my job to keep him in check."

Before Dylan could respond, Jena came out of the dressing room wearing the miniskirt Megan had chosen for her. She looked stunning.

Matt let his eyes drift down to her long legs. Now there were two things that had captured his attention—the boots and the miniskirt.

"Hey, baby." Eric grabbed Megan and kissed her. "I see you're having fun helping Miss Taylor."

"I am," Megan said as Scott put his arm around her shoulder. "Jena, I'd like to introduce you to my guys. This one is Eric." She kissed him on the cheek. Then she did the same to her other man. "And this is Scott."

He looked at Jena and saw her tremble.

"I'm so sorry," she said. "I really thought I was dealing with you, Mr. Knight, not Kip."

"You are now," Scott said. "With your help and these two Texans, we'll get the bastard. I'm sure of it."

"Damn right," Eric added.

"I'll do my best," she told them. "Megan, I've loved shopping with you, but I think it's time to get to work on the code right now. The sooner we do, the sooner we can get Mitrofanov and Lunceford."

"Not on an empty stomach," Matt said, placing his arm around her just like Scott had done with Megan. It felt right to hold her this way. She was his and Sean's. It would take time to convince her of that fact, but however long it took, he and Sean would take it. He wanted her. Always.

"Listen to your man," Megan said. "You've got to try a burger at Lucy's."

Matt's stomach growled. "They're the best I've ever tasted. Let's go eat."

"Only if you promise we can go to TBK and get cracking on Kip's virus right after."

Scott shook his head. "First thing in the morning is soon enough. We all need a break. Besides, Megan wants to throw you a party, Jena, to welcome you to Destiny."

"A party?" Jena looked shocked. "For me?"

"Scott Knight, you blew my surprise." Megan shook her head. "Yes, a party. We love parties in Destiny, and any excuse to throw one is always welcome. Everyone wants to meet you."

"I don't understand. How did you pull one together on such short notice? I just got here yesterday." Jena's eyes were wide but the cute little smile on her face thrilled Matt.

"Gretchen can do just about anything." Megan walked next to Jena. "Besides, Destonians are capable of doing magic when they want to. And for you, we all want to throw you a big shindig."

He could tell Jena was still holding back. Was it because she was afraid to get in too deep with Destiny, with him, with Sean? She'd confessed to running from her ex, the guy who had killed her father. It might be hard for her to stop running. He and Sean knew a thing or two about running. Until they'd enlisted into the military, running had been their whole life.

"Honey, the Knights are our bosses," he told her. "Don't make us look bad, okay?"

"Okay," she said. "I guess I'm going to a party tonight. What in the world shall I wear?" she teased. "I just don't have a thing to choose from."

She and Megan laughed.

Sean put his arm around her and he carried her new clothes out to the car.

We've got to sit down with her and talk. She needs to know our story and how we feel about her.

* * * *

Matt sat on the couch, watching ESPN. Actually he wasn't watching it. His mind was racing about Jena. She was still getting ready for Megan's party. He felt like the luckiest man in the world. The most beautiful, wonderful woman turned out to be Robin Hood. She'd been through hell, but never gave up. She survived and made sure her daughter and mother remained safe from a psychopath. That fucker didn't know what was coming for him. He and Sean would take care of that guy once and for all for Jena.

God, Jena. She was brilliant, loyal, and loved her daughter with all her heart. He never dreamed he would find someone as perfect as her for him and Sean.

"How about a cold one, bro?" Sean asked.

He nodded, keeping his gaze on the television. "Don't mind if I do."

Sean handed him the beer. "You seem to be looking at a blank screen. Bet you don't have a clue what they're saying."

"You read me like a book. My mind was on Jena and all that she told us about her life. I want to protect her in every way possible. She's been through enough and now it's time for us to share that burden."

"I don't want her to feel alone ever again. We're both here for her, but it's time to tell her about our life." Sean took a long drink of his beer. "We need her complete trust."

"There couldn't be two men more alike than we are, buddy." Matt put his hand on his best friend's shoulder. "That same thought crossed my mind, too."

"Whenever the time is right, let's make that a priority, the sooner, the better," Sean said. "I love the fact she has a daughter."

"I know," he sighed. "I can fully understand why she was so motivated in all that she did. Her mom and daughter mean the world to her."

Sean nodded. "She's too good for us, but I will never let her go."

"I totally agree. She's the best thing that has happened to us and we want her safe and happy."

"Let's put all our cards on the table for her. It can only make us closer."

"I hope I'm not jumping the gun, Sean, but I can see you and I finally having a real family."

Chapter Ten

In between Matt and Sean, Jena walked up to the big double doors of the mansion.

Megan had told her people in Destiny liked to throw a party, but this was a much bigger turnout than she imagined. The cars outside the place lined not only the driveway, but also the entire street. How many people were here? At least a hundred.

She was a little anxious, but she vowed to herself not to show it. "Surely this isn't just for me."

Matt shrugged. "Let's find out." He knocked on the door.

It opened and an elderly woman in a traditional maid's outfit appeared. "Welcome to Knight Mansion, Miss Taylor." Her English accent was endearing. "Please come in."

"Gretchen, you look wonderful tonight." Sean leaned down and kissed the woman on the cheek.

"You're a devil, Mr. MacCabe," Gretchen said with a wink.

They walked in. Jena looked up at the banner strung across the impressive foyer. It said *Welcome, Jena, to Destiny!*

"Oh my God. This really is for me?"

"Yes it is," Megan said, stepping up with her two fiancés, Eric and Scott. The crowd that had gathered in the space applauded. "Everyone is anxious to meet you, Jena."

"You've done so much for me already. I'm stunned by this."

"Then you better fasten your seat belt, because there's more to come." Megan handed her a yellow rose. "This is from me and my guys. I'm so glad to have you as my friend, Jena."

"You're the best one I've ever had." She hugged Megan, feeling overcome with happiness. Tears welled in her eyes.

Gretchen came up beside her with a large vase. "Miss Taylor, you'll need this for your flowers."

"But I only have one."

"Every family in Destiny is going to give you a welcome flower. It was Ethel's idea. The Irish can be so dramatic at times."

"I'm not Irish, and you know it." Another woman, about the same age as Gretchen, came up beside her with two men in tow. "Don't listen to her, Jena," the sweet lady said with a grin. "She's a troublemaker. I'm Ethel O'Leary and these are my handsome husbands, Patrick and Sam. They *are* Irish."

Both Ethel's husbands were very nice-looking gentlemen.

Patrick smiled. "Nice to meet you, young lady."

"Welcome to our town, Miss Taylor."

She shook their hands. "Please call me Jena."

"My men might be from the Emerald Isle but I'm from Missouri."

"You married them, Ethel," Gretchen winked. "That makes you Irish in my book."

"I know," she shot back. It was clear these two women were fond of each other. Ethel handed Jena another rose. "This is for you."

She took the pink flower. "Thank you. This is beautiful. I'm so happy to meet you. This is quite the town."

"What do you think of our dragon statues in the park?" Patrick asked.

"Don't you dare start with your stories." Ethel kissed him. "This is a party. Give the girl a chance to enjoy herself before you scare her off with your imaginary dragons."

"They are hardly imaginary, sweetheart."

"Listen to our wife, Patrick. There are other people who want to meet Jena," Sam said.

Patrick leaned forward. "Another time. You look like someone with an open mind to me."

"I can't wait to hear all about it," she told him. The three of them were adorable. She wondered how long they'd been together.

Wearing sunglasses, Dylan Strange came up with Erica and Cameron.

Erica handed her a red rose. "I'm so glad to see you again. Dylan keeps going on and on about how brave you were in Odessa."

"That's high praise from my brother," Cameron added. "He rarely gives compliments. Told me and our lovely bride that you were also quite the driver, too."

"Red is my favorite color." She placed the stem into the vase with the other two. "Thank you."

Erica leaned in and whispered. "I know this is a little overwhelming, but you'll come to love our town. I promise."

"I'm already crazy about it," she confessed.

"Crazy is good in Destiny," Cam said with a laugh.

As the Stranges stepped aside, Jena saw a line had formed behind them. She looked at Matt and Sean, who remained on either side of her. This felt almost like a receiving line at a wedding, though she'd never been a bride herself. God, was there any place on earth like this place? She doubted there was.

Sheriff Jason Wolfe stepped up with two other men she didn't recognize. She'd seen him at the boutique that Megan had taken her to earlier that day, but tonight he was not in uniform. The man was quite handsome, as were the duo next to him.

Jason handed her a peach-colored rose. "Welcome, Jena. These are my two brothers, Mitchell and Lucas."

"Thank you for the rose. I'm so glad to meet you." She was surprised that they didn't have a woman with them.

As Jason, Mitchell, and Lucas moved aside, Matt leaned in. "Those three are so lovesick for Phoebe Blue. She's the one in the red dress about three families back in line."

"As good looking as the three Wolfe brothers are, I'm surprised the woman isn't with them."

"We don't know the whole story," Sean whispered, "but

apparently it has something to do with Jason sending her brother Shane to prison a few years back."

"That would be a tough hurdle to get over." She noticed that Phoebe was sneaking peeks at the Wolfe brothers. "I think she might be a little lovesick, too."

More people handed her flowers until Gretchen had to bring her another vase. There had to be at least fifty roses she'd been given already. What a welcome. Everyone in Destiny was so sweet and kind to her.

Megan returned to her side when the last family had given her their flower.

"I still am overwhelmed you did this for me. I don't know what to say."

"Tell me you will come to my wedding."

"I would love to," Jena answered, doubting she could. To keep her own family safe, she had to keep moving, running. "When is it?"

"Day after tomorrow."

"What? You're kidding."

"Nope. I'm so excited. You will come, won't you?"

"Of course. How in the world did you pull this off when your own wedding is so soon?"

Megan pointed to some of the women around the room. "I had help, Jena. One thing I've learned since coming to Destiny, you're never alone. I have my guys and I also have my dear, sweet friends." Megan took her hands and squeezed. "I'd like us to be friends, too."

"Me, too." *I wish it was possible but it isn't.*

The band fired up a song.

Matt and Sean led her to the ballroom. The floor was packed with people dancing. Along the walls were tables of delicious food. No one had ever done anything like this for her.

Megan and her men had thrown her this party even after all she'd done to their company.

Matt and Sean spun her around the dance floor until she was out of breath. What a night. One she would never forget.

"I need to sit for a minute," she told them.

"Do you want something to drink?" Sean asked her.

"Just a glass of water, please."

Matt leaned down and kissed her on the cheek. "I'll bring us some food to nibble on. The Knights always put out the best spread."

"You guys spoil me."

"Our pleasure, sweetheart," he said.

Sean nodded and stroked her hair. "Yes, it is our pleasure. Every second of it." He scanned the room. "You'll be safe here."

"I agree." Matt's gaze circled the space, too. "Only Destonians present."

"I'm not helpless, fellows." She patted her purse. "I have my own gun."

"She's a tough one, our girl, isn't she?" Sean asked Matt.

"Very true. Let's go. She'll be ready to scoot her boots when we get back."

Jena watched them walk to get food and drink.

Reaching into her purse, she pulled out the burner phone and dialed her mom.

As much as she would love to stay in Destiny with Matt and Sean, she knew that was an impossible dream. Leaving would be hard. She'd already told them everything. They would understand why she had to go. Staying in one place for too long would be dangerous for her, for her mom, and for Kimmie. Carl was still out there, waiting.

* * * *

With a towel around his waist, Sean sat at his kitchen table, sipping on a beer. Jena's two vases with all the roses she'd been given tonight were on the counter by the window. She was cleaning up in one bathroom and Matt was showering in the other.

What a night. Jena had seemed to enjoy most of the evening.

When he and Matt had returned with drink and food, he noticed a stark change in her. She was guarded again and asked to leave shortly after.

They'd said their good-byes and returned to the house.

She's holding back. Why?

Was she worried about her kid or her ex or both?

She came out of the bathroom wearing silk pajamas she'd gotten during her shopping spree with Megan. God, what a gorgeous woman Jena was. Her hair was wrapped up in a towel. Green eyes gazed at him, imploring him to help her.

"Come have a beer with me, sweetheart." He would move heaven and earth to make her happy.

She nodded and sat down in the chair next to him. They remained together quietly for a couple of minutes and then Matt joined them.

He put his arm around her. "What's troubling you?"

"You both seem to be able to see right through me. I am so grateful for all you've done. Everyone in Destiny seems so wonderful. I can see why you two have decided to stay. I just can't."

"Can't what?" Matt asked. "You can't stay with us?"

"Not just you two. I can't stay here in Destiny. I told you about Carl. He's dangerous."

Sean could see the suffering in her eyes. How much had she endured because of that fucker?

She continued, her voice softer than before. "I'm willing to stay here for three more days and then I have to leave for Kimmie's birthday. Afterward, my mom, Kimmie, and I will disappear again."

"Baby, we will go with you," Matt said. "We'll bring them back here. This place is big enough for all of us. If it proves to be too small, we'll get a new place. You belong with us."

She shook her head. "I wish I could. I really do. But I have to think about what's good for my daughter. She's first in all my decisions." Jena reached into one of the pockets of her PJs and brought out a photo. "I wanted to show you a picture of Kimmie." She handed it to Matt. "She's the light of my life."

"She's beautiful, like her mother." Matt passed the photo over to him.

He looked at the smiling, red-haired little girl in the picture, whose eyes were as green as Jena's, and felt a protective tug on his heart. Who could harm such a sweet, innocent child? "Leave it to me and Matt, Jena. We'll find Carl and make sure he never bothers you and Kimmie again."

"If only you were right. But the police haven't found him, and until they do, I can't risk Kimmie's safety. Carl is evil. He blames me for his incarceration. I know it doesn't make sense. But that's how he thinks. Crazy. He will never rest until he finds me, so I have to keep running. Can you understand that?"

"We understand more than you know, Jena," Matt said.

Sean looked at his best friend. "It's time."

Matt nodded. "I agree. She deserves to know all of it."

She'd trusted them with her story. Maybe telling her theirs would make her see that she belonged with them. Together they could make sure Jena, her mom, and Kimmie stayed safe and away from Carl. That son of a bitch was going back to prison or six feet under. He and Matt would make sure of that.

She sighed and took a sip of her beer. "What do I need to know?"

He put his hand at the back of her neck and pulled her mouth to his. "Jena, I love you."

"I love you, too, but—"

"Wait, baby." Matt leaned in and kissed her, staking his claim on the woman of their dreams. "I love you. I will always love you."

"I love you, Matt. I love you, Sean. But I can't let my heart take over here. Kimmie is my baby. She needs me to be the best mom I can be. I have to leave. I have to do everything I can to keep her safe."

Sean removed her towel from her head. Her damp red locks fell to her shoulders. "Honey, I hate what you've had to deal with. It's too much for anyone. And you did it all on your own. Matt and I know a thing or two about that. I know you believe you should leave. Running has been your life for far too long. But you don't have to run anymore."

Jena stood. "I can't ask you to do this. It's too much." She ran to the bedroom before they could stop her.

Chapter Eleven

With tears streaming down her cheeks, Jena closed the door. She wasn't about to take all the outfits Megan had bought for her. She went to the closet and brought out the clothes she'd been wearing the day she'd met Matt and Sean.

The last few days with the two Texans had been the best in her life. That's why this was so hard. Looking at them around their kitchen table sipping beer felt so right. She belonged here—with them. But it just couldn't be.

I don't want my hell to be their hell. They have no idea what Carl is capable of. I do.

I must do what is best. Oh God, this is so hard. I love them. I love them with my whole being. I wish there was another way, but I know Carl would kill them. I simply can't let that happen. I must go. There is no other answer. Please, God, help me. I can't bring myself to do this without your help.

There was a quick knock at the door and Matt and Sean walked in.

"We're here." Matt grabbed her hand and squeezed. "Baby, what's wrong? We're here for you. For Kimmie. For your mom. You're not alone anymore."

Sean caressed her cheeks and gently wiped her eyes. "You are the family we never had."

"What do you mean the family you never had?" She saw pain in both their eyes that broke her heart.

"Sean and I have known each other all our lives," Matt told her. "He's like a brother to me."

"Same here." Sean nodded. "We *are* brothers. After all we've been through, no two men could be tighter than we are. Our parents were involved in a cult."

That revelation shocked her.

"That's putting it mildly, bro." Matt turned to her. The intense seriousness in his demeanor was something she hadn't seen before. "They were completely lost to this creepy guy who called himself *The Enlightened One*."

"He also went by Reverend William Mayfield but he made his followers call him Brother," Sean added.

"Do you mean the same Brother Willie who was the leader of the group in Belco, Mississippi?" She'd read about the cult leader in a sociology class at MIT.

"The one and only," Sean said. "I was born in the commune. My parents were with the asshole from the very beginning."

"My parents came later. About two years before the FBI raid." Matt was calm, as if what he was telling her was as common as a hot summer day in Texas. But it wasn't common. Far from it. "Willie thought he was the embodiment of God on earth. As kids, we had to kneel to him whenever he came in the room."

She wanted to hold them both. "Everything I read about the man said he was a monster."

"On every level, Jena." Matt sighed. "My sister was only three. They never found her remains in the fire. For a long time I held onto the dream that Carrie was alive. When I was at the CIA, I used every resource I could to find her." He closed his eyes. "She's gone. I have to accept that."

"I'm so sorry." Jena put her arm around him. "I thought everyone died that day except the cult leader."

Matt's tone hardened. "We're the only survivors besides that fucker. The authorities kept our names out of the papers. We were taken into protective custody and eventually were farmed out to an orphanage."

"How did you two get out of the compound before it burned

down?"

"When the shooting started, Matt and I ran into Willie's office, still thinking the bastard could do something miraculous to save us and our parents." Sean's voice was steady, but she could tell the memories he and Matt were sharing held great pain. "The asshole was gone. At first, I thought he'd vanished back into heaven. The damn lying fucker had brainwashed all of us. Matt found the trap door to a secret tunnel."

"We crawled back to get our parents and my sister to tell them about the escape route," Matt continued. "That's when we saw all the parents, including ours, shooting not at the agents outside, but at one another."

"Children were killed first." Sean lowered his head.

"Oh my God," she said.

"My dad spotted me and aimed his gun at my head. That's when some of the women set fire to the drapes using gasoline. A spark hit my dad's shirt before he could fire his gun. Matt and I ran back to Willie's office and scrambled down the tunnel."

Matt looked at her with unblinking eyes. "Thirty-seven adults died and twelve children."

She wept for them, for their suffering, for the loss of their innocence. She could see the men they'd become, but in her mind's eye she saw the two boys, about Kimmie's age, clutching each other as their insane parents went up in flames. She'd been older when her dad had died in the car crash. She remembered standing on the track watching his vehicle's fiery explosion. In a strange way, what she shared with Matt and Sean, losing their parents in fire, deepened her connection to them.

She kissed them, again and again, through teary eyes. They knew pain. Deep pain. What she had with them now was unbreakable. Leaving them and Destiny was no longer possible.

"You're a true mother to Kimmie. You've seen hell. So have we." Sean pulled her into his arms. "We survived. You will, too."

"We won't let you down, Jena." Matt joined the embrace, squeezing her. "We won't fail you. We will keep you, Kimmie, and your mom safe." He leaned over and gave her a romantic kiss—soft, sweet, tender.

Although she felt tingles, it was a kiss like no other. A forever kiss.

He released her and Sean touched her on the cheek. She turned to him and, like Matt, he sealed their lips together in a silent vow of commitment. These two men were her life now. She was no longer alone. Never before had she felt so secure about her life and her future, about Kimmie's and her mom's safety. For the first time, they had protectors—men who would put them first. Always.

"We lost everything that day, Jena," Sean said. "Now, we have a family again. With you."

Matt smiled. "You're our family, baby."

She knew Matt and Sean wanted her, and their lives would be together from now on.

"I love you, guys."

"I love you, sweetheart." Sean stood, gazing down at her with so much love in his eyes it made her tingle.

Matt lifted her into his arms. "I love you, baby." Carrying her to the bed, he kissed her the entire way.

Gently placing her on the bed, Matt stepped back, clearly making room for his friend Sean.

Their bond amazed her.

Sean bent down and kissed her tenderly. "Baby, you've made me so happy. I never dreamed I would be so lucky."

She touched his chin and felt his manly stubble. "Me either. I can't believe I found you two wonderful Texans."

"We actually found you, sweetheart," Matt teased, flinging his towel to the side with the flair she'd come to love in him. "In Odessa. Or have you forgotten, my little Robin Hood?"

She smiled. "I haven't forgotten a thing, Mr. Tall Texan."

"That's good."

"We want to make sure you never forget." Sean unbuttoned the top of her pajamas, exposing her breasts. "My God, I don't think I'll ever get over how beautiful you are." His hands gently caressed her mounds, causing warmth to spread through her body.

"I can't believe how beautiful you are either." She moved her fingertips to Sean's muscled chest.

Matt pulled her bottoms off and crawled up between her legs. "Everything about you is perfection, baby." His gaze locked on her eyes, though his hot mouth was just inches away from her pussy. "I don't deserve you, but I will never let you go. I will spend the rest of my life showing you how much you mean to me. You're my world, Jena."

"You're my heaven and earth, Matt. You and Sean." She tugged on Sean's towel.

He grinned and flung it to the floor.

Matt lowered his mouth onto her most intimate flesh. She inhaled a deep, devoted breath as Sean began licking and sucking her nipples. In all her life, she'd never felt so completely and utterly loved—totally wanted. She desperately hoped they knew how much she loved them. Unconditionally.

She reached for Sean's cock and Matt's hair, stroking them, letting her fingers speak for her. Her nipples throbbed from Sean's fingers and lips and her pussy was wet from Matt's mouth and tongue. Their lovemaking had always been wonderful, but her tingles now carried so much more. Every shiver said "I love you." Every quake, "You are mine." Excitement expanded inside her with the joy of their sweet caresses on her body. Heat rolled through her like a wildfire. The pressure was building fast, brought on by the passion of her two men.

Matt kissed her thighs tenderly, igniting an electrifying line that went from his lips to her nipples, where Sean's mouth remained, and back again to her soaked pussy.

Sean shifted down her one side and Matt came up her other. They both kissed their way along her body, one up and one down, switching positions.

Sean's hot breath skated across her swollen folds. Matt's breath blew across her hard nipples.

She, too, switched positions, reaching for Matt's hard cock and Sean's soft hair. Sex had never felt so deep, so connected, so perfect to her. Every kiss, caress, and lick was more than just play. All they were doing to her was sealing her heart to them forever. Warm dizziness lifted her up until she felt like she was floating. *God, how I love them. My heart is theirs.*

She tugged on Sean's hair and Matt's cock. "I need to taste both of you. Please get on each side of me."

They both smiled and came to the top of the bed on either side of her. Their cocks were rock hard and straight up. Leaning forward, she took hold of both of them. She offered her mouth to Matt and then to Sean. Her lips were throbbing like mad as she went back and forth, enjoying their manly kisses. As she stroked their shafts, their kisses deepened, filled with fiery hunger.

"Please get on your backs for me."

They nodded and went into the perfect position for her to enjoy.

Continuing to kiss and stroke her men, she shifted her body on the center of the mattress, lying on her stomach with her head facing the foot of the bed.

Kissing the tip of Matt's cock, she tightened her grip on Sean's dick.

Matt lifted her left leg and began licking her pussy, causing her clit to throb.

She circled her tongue over the slit at the top of Matt's cock and drank down the pearly drop she found there. Sean's loving hands wandered over her body, making her tingle from head to toe.

Swallowing Matt's dick, she began stroking Sean's cock. The manly groans that came from their lips thrilled her. She removed her lips from Matt, but kept hold of him with her hands. She turned her head to Sean and tasted his cock with her tongue, shifting her body to him. Sean lifted her right leg and kissed her mound tenderly. Taking as much as she could of his ten-inch cock down her throat, she felt him grab her clit between his lips, causing her need to expand and burn.

"I want to make love to you, baby." Matt said. "I want to be inside you, to feel you, to be one."

"I want that, too," she confessed. "More than anything. I want you both." She crawled on top of Matt and took his cock, placing it inside her body. Leaning back, she moved rhythmically. Feeling Matt inside enflamed her.

She turned to Sean, who was on his knees with his dick in front of her mouth. She swallowed him, drinking down as much of his erection as she could. Matt thrust into her, driving her mad with desire. She could feel Sean's big hands on her hair, tugging slightly.

The deeper Matt drove into her, the more she felt her pressure build. She released Sean's cock with her lips, replacing them with her fingers.

"I'm so fucking close." He growled.

"Please. Yes. God." Her passion-filled words flew out of her with every breath. Staring into Matt's hazel eyes, she felt herself pulsating. His face tightened, his eyelids narrowed, and he shoved his cock deep into her pussy.

Feeling him come inside her sent her over the edge. She climaxed like never before. A flood of sensations captured every nerve ending. She leaned forward and kissed Matt as her womb spasmed around his cock.

Continuing to ride the release, Sean took over, pulling her off of Matt and placing her on the mattress facing him. "You're ours, Jena. Both of ours."

"I am yours. And you and Matt are mine," she whispered back, feeling the connection between her and her men deepen.

Sean thrust his cock into her, in and out, and the pressure began to build anew inside her.

Matt caressed her body and stroked her hair as Sean filled her completely, hitting that perfect spot that drove her mad with desire.

The overwhelming friction in her pussy from his cock helped her reach another climax.

"Yes," she panted. "Oh God."

"Fuck." Sean's body tensed as he shot his load into her depths.

As they all started to relax, a multitude of shivers took hold of her. This was by far the most intimate sex she'd ever experienced in her whole life. "I love you so much," she told them.

"I love you, Robin Hood," Matt said, kissing her trembling lips.

When he released her, Sean took hold of her mouth. "I love you, Jena."

Chapter Twelve

Matt looked over at the clock, which shined the time in blue numerals.

6:00 a.m.

Sean headed quietly for the door, motioning he would bring back coffee for them.

He nodded his approval. Sean left and Jena remained asleep.

On his elbows in the bed, Matt gazed down at her, her lips slightly open, allowing warm breaths to escape.

God, she's beautiful.

He should be tired, but he wasn't. Not one damn bit. Making love to Jena with Sean had been like nothing he'd ever experienced. He and Sean had shared before, but what had happened last night changed everything. She was theirs. He had no doubt about it now.

His life had never been better. The reason? Jena. She'd brought light to Sean and him.

Jena had spunk and fire he enjoyed. And deep down, in the core of her being, was devotion so strong, so unshakable, it called to his heart. She loved her daughter and had sacrificed everything to make sure Kimmie remained safe. Her mother, too.

The little girl in the picture that Jena had shown them would be part of his and Sean's lives. He'd never met Kimmie, but he would do anything for her. She was Jena's. That was enough for him. Being a dad was something he'd never thought he would do given what kind of upbringing he'd gone through. But now, after meeting and falling in love with Jena, he wanted to be the best he could be for Kimmie.

The only family he'd ever been able to really count on had been

Sean. That was, until finding Jena. Their lives had been reborn because of her.

He took a deep breath.

They would need to call Mr. Black to find out whatever was in the systems about Jena's ex, Carl Braxton. Black was the best in the CIA. If there was any information out there, he would get it.

Sean stepped back into the bedroom. He held a tray with a coffee pot, three cups, cream, and sugar.

"She's still asleep," he said quietly, trying not to disturb her.

"I'm not surprised," Sean said in a hushed tone, placing the coffee on the nightstand. "We had quite the time last night."

"That we did."

Sean filled two of the cups and handed one of them to him. "When I was making coffee, I called Black."

"And?"

"He patched Dylan into the call," Sean said. "Black is putting a team together to see what he can find out on Braxton."

"With him on it, we'll find the fucker. No one can hide forever." He took a sip of coffee. "You and I both know that."

"You know what?" Jena asked with a yawn.

"Don't trouble your head over it, baby," he told her. She had enough to worry about already.

She sat up and stared at him. "After all we talked about last night, don't go clamming up on me now, Mr. Matt Dixon."

"She's got you on the ropes," Sean teased.

"And you, Mr. Sean MacCabe. You're just as bad as he is. I'm a big girl. Please don't hold back from me. Secrets have been my life for the past few years. Very necessary, of course, but I'd like it to be different with you two."

"It will be." Matt leaned into her and captured her lips. "Actually, it *is* different already. For us, too, baby. We've never been in a serious relationship before."

"Is that what this is?" She smiled. "A serious relationship?"

"You know it is, Jena." Sean kissed her. "The truth is we're working with an old friend in the Agency to find Carl Braxton."

"Thank you." She closed her eyes, and he could almost sense the weight she'd been carrying lessen a bit. God, he hoped so. "Do you think your friend will be successful?"

He loved how direct she could be. "Black is about the best there is. Besides, you have Dylan Strange and us on the case, too. We won't rest until the son of a bitch is found. We've never failed any mission and we won't fail this time. We won't fail you."

Her smile thrilled him.

"Would you like some coffee, sweetheart," Sean asked her.

"Yes, please." She took the fresh cup of coffee that Sean had just poured. "You even brought cream."

"I did. Sugar, too."

"Just cream." She poured some into her cup and took a sip. "Perfect."

"You hungry?" Matt asked.

She giggled. "You and your bottomless pit stomach. Sean, the grocery bill has got to be crazy."

"One of the biggest," his best friend said with a laugh.

"What about you? You're just as bad as me." He turned to Jena and touched her cheek. "The longer you're around him, you'll see I'm right. He's just putting his best foot forward."

"I'm sure there's a ton to learn about you two." She grinned. "Two boyfriends. I never dreamed of such a thing."

"Dreams sometimes just fall in your lap, baby." Sean poured a cup of coffee for himself.

"Seems so. I have some questions, fellows. Lots of questions."

"Fire away," Matt told her, enjoying being in bed next to her drinking coffee. They were all so relaxed, as if they'd been doing this every morning for years.

"Guys, we are talking about a future, right?" she asked. "I mean a forever future."

Matt gazed into her green eyes. "I know one thing." He kissed her tenderly on the lips. "I will never leave you, Jena."

"You took the words out of my mouth, buddy." Sean leaned into Jena. "You are mine. You are his. You are ours. And we are yours. Got it?" Sean pressed his mouth to hers. "Now that we've found you, we won't ever let you go."

"I don't want you to. I want to be here with you. But this is fast. You both have to know that, too."

"Fast doesn't mean it isn't right, sweetheart," Matt told her.

"I know. My mom and dad only knew each other eight days before they eloped. They were so in love. Soul mates in every way."

"Do you have any brothers or sisters?" Sean asked.

"I'm an only child. They wanted more and tried, according to my mom, but all they got was me."

"Why try again when you get perfection on the first go-round?" Matt asked even though he knew it would've been better for her to have had a brother or sister to carry some of the load. He wasn't sure what would've happened to him if he hadn't had Sean by his side.

"Would Kimmie like a brother or sister?" Sean asked.

She nodded. "Which brings me to my next question. If this does turn out to be forever—"

"It will," he interjected, hoping to drive the point home. "This *is* forever."

"I know," she kissed his cheek. "What about children? How will that work?"

"It'll be the luckiest child in the world," Sean told her.

"Two dads who will shower them with love," he added. "Plus, they will have the most wonderful mother. Look what you've done for Kimmie. You've put her first."

"Always." She took a deep breath.

"And we don't want to leave out your mom," Sean said. "How lucky will Kimmie and our new babies be to have their grandmother living in the same house?"

"Are you saying you two won't care which one of you is the father?"

"I don't give a damn. Mine? Matt's? That isn't how it will be," Sean said the words that were on his mind.

"We might be two people, but we share everything," he told her. "We've had to, Jena. You heard what we've been through. Biology won't change a thing when it comes to our babies. They will be ours, just like you, just like Kimmie."

"This all sounds wonderful, guys, but I still am not sure how I'm going to break this to my mom. She's from a different era."

"Maybe so, but she is your mom," Sean said.

Matt stroked her hair. "I bet she's tough as nails."

"She is tough. Very." She set down her empty cup.

"She's probably one of the most understanding people around." He grabbed her hand and squeezed. "You, your mom, and Kimmie have had to suffer through so much, but you did it together. If you're anything like your mother, which I'm certain you are, she only wants you to be safe and happy. Right?"

"That does sound like her. She's given up everything for me and Kimmie."

He cupped her chin. "I don't think there will be a problem then, sweetheart. This is not only forever. This is happily ever after, princess."

"Okay, Master," she said. "Which brings me to my next question. How does someone join the club? You are members, right?"

He smiled and turned to Sean, who was also beaming. "Yes. We're members." God, Jena was the cutest thing ever. "Why do you ask?"

"You know. You promised to show me some things about the BDSM lifestyle." The sweet little vixen smiled. "How about now?"

"Well, okay then," Sean answered. "This is the best way to start the day."

"Be right back." Matt leapt from the bed, excited at the prospect of continuing her training. He went into the sex closet, as he and Sean had dubbed it. *This needs to be mild. We've only shown her a little of the lifestyle.* He grabbed a paddle, handcuffs, and a vibrator.

When he got back to the bedroom, Sean already had Jena out of the bed and on her knees.

His cock stirred at the sight.

Sean looked at him. "I was telling this newbie submissive about some of the protocols."

"Excellent." He walked behind her, placing the toys on the bed. "Tell me what you know so far, sub."

"Yes, Sir. Master Sean was reminding me about my safe words." She fired off a pretty good definition of what they were.

"Very good." He stroked her hair, tugging on it slightly. "Look at me."

She gazed at him with her green eyes. Her cheeks were flush and her breasts were heaving. She was into this and that made him even harder.

"At the core of this lifestyle is trust. Everything about it hinges on that. Tops must earn their bottoms' trust, but it is a two-way street. There is no scene that is better than any other scene. Some Doms and subs play only a step or two above vanilla, but they still have wonderful sex lives and long-lasting relationships."

"I'm ready, Matt." She pursed her lips. Her impatience was going to get her into trouble. "I get how this works. Let's get on with it."

"No, you don't." He reached down and pinched her nipples. "You have no clue."

Her eyes widened, and her lips thinned. But she didn't say a word.

He smiled, releasing her tiny buds. "Silence. Very good."

"She's got the heart of a sub," Sean said. "And the body of a goddess."

"Try to hold back on the compliments, bro. This one has a whole heap of defiance we're going to have to work on." He bent down so that their eyes were locked, making sure to keep his body slightly above her. "I pinched your nipples to get your attention, baby. You made two errors. One, you called me by name. When we're in play or a scene, that won't be tolerated. You may refer to me as Sir or Master. To differentiate between Sean and me you may add our names after. For instance, you may call me Sir Matt or Master Matt. Got it?"

"Yes, Master Matt."

"Two, you tried to take charge. I won't let you get away with that. Understand?"

She nodded, but he could see the fire in her eyes.

"You still want this, don't you? Us to train you? To show you about our lifestyle?"

"Yes, Sir. I do."

He knew she was telling the truth, but sensed her old habits of self-protection remained. Building up her trust for him would be his pleasure.

"Now, where was I?" He looked at the time and realized he needed to hurry things along. They needed to be at TBK by nine this morning. "You don't have to know the entire history of BDSM or even all the protocols right now, but Sean and I decide what happens and what doesn't, understand?"

"Yes, Sir."

"Better." He turned to Sean. "Shall I spank her pretty bottom or shall you?"

Out of the corner of his eye he saw her fingers curl into tiny fists of rebelliousness. *God, this is going to be so fun with her.*

"She disrespected you, Matt. I think it is only right for you to punish her."

Her hand went up, making her look even cuter.

Sean laughed. "Looks like our sub has a question."

"Yes, it does." He lifted her up into his arms. He wanted to kiss her. He knew he shouldn't, but couldn't help himself, pressing his lips to hers. "What do you want to ask?"

"I didn't mean to disrespect you, Master. I'm sorry."

"That's not your question, is it?"

"No. Are you going to spank me…Sir?" she asked, her tone almost giddy.

"Already topping from the bottom and we haven't even really begun. You are going to be a handful, sweetheart." He sat down on the bed, keeping a firm hold on her. "Yes, I'm going to spank you. You must understand who is in charge and although you're sorry, you haven't quite learned your lesson. But you will. I'll make sure of that." He flipped her around so that her bottom was in the best position. He grabbed the paddle. It was dark blue with holes in it. "What state are you in, sub? What color?"

"Green, Sir."

He swung the paddle and connected it to her gorgeous ass twice. "Who is in charge?"

"Matt and Sean," she answered incorrectly.

He smacked her sweet flesh again. "Who?"

"You and Sean, of course."

Sean shook his head. "I know you can't see it, Matt, but this naughty girl is smiling."

He grinned. God, Jena was the best thing that had ever happened to him, but he needed to remain strong. This was her first sample of BDSM. He couldn't get off on the wrong foot.

He slapped the paddle to her ass harder and heard her gasp.

"I mean Master Matt and Sir Sean," she said quickly.

"Damn right we are." He stood, lifting her into his arms again. "Time to learn how to get pleasure from us, baby." He lowered her back onto the mattress. Seeing her lying there, naked and exposed for him and Sean, got his pulse burning. "Color?"

"Green. Very green." The sass in her tone was still there. "Very green…Sir."

"Sean, why don't you use the vibrator on her and remind her again how that, too, can be used by us to earn her submission."

"My pleasure." Sean got the vibrator and turned it on. The whole room seemed to hum, but he knew it was only the toy. "What do you call me, sub?"

"What would you like me to call you?"

Sean turned off the vibrator. "I'll ask you again. What do you call me?"

She stared at the toy with passion-filled eyes. "Master Sean or Sir Sean."

Sean flipped the vibrator back on and brought it to her inner thigh. "How does that feel?"

"Good. So good." Her hands shot down to her pussy.

Sean removed the device. "Good? Don't you have more to say, sub."

"Sir. Yes, Sir." Her fingers threaded through her wet folds. "So good, Sir."

"Sean, hold up a second." He grabbed her by the wrists and pulled her hands off her pussy. "That's our job, baby. Not yours. Don't touch what is ours. Got it?"

She nodded so sweetly, causing his lust to go into overdrive. God, how he wanted to take her right then, to send his dick into her pussy, to fill her with his seed.

He gazed at her. "Who is in charge?"

"You are, Sir. You and Master Sean."

"Damn right we are," he repeated, driving the point home. He put the cuffs on her wrists and placed her arms above her head until her hands touched the headboard. "Keep them here, got it."

"Yes, Sir."

He smiled. "Very good. Now you're getting it." He bent down and sucked on her breasts as Sean sent the vibrator back to her pussy.

She moaned, which thrilled him.

"Who is in charge?"

"You are, Master. You and Master Sean."

"Damn right." He teethed her nipples and felt her trembles on his lips. He moved his hands all over her body, enjoying the feel of her silky skin.

"More, Master Matt, more."

He pinched her nipples a little harder than before.

Sean removed the toy. "You're being naughty again, sub. We'll decide when you have more."

He licked her neck. "You must learn to obey."

"I will, Sirs. I promise, but please don't stop touching me. I can't stand not to be touched by you."

He liked her pleading, knowing her need was getting the better of her. That was just how he wanted her. "You want to come?"

"Yes. Please."

"You can't. We are in control of that, too. You must trust us to know when to end your suffering."

"But I'm dying. It's so much."

"And guess what, sub? It's going to be even more. Lucky for you, the more we withhold your climax, the better it will be."

"Oh God," she breathed, curling her fingers in the cuffs.

He bathed her nipples again and Sean sent the vibrator into her pussy.

"Yes. Green. Yes, Sirs. Green. I'm green. Please don't stop, Sirs. Please. Green. Really green."

He laughed as she freely offered the color without being prompted. "Should we let our sweet sub come, Sean?"

"I think she's earned it." Sean turned up the speed on the vibrator.

"I do, too." He tweaked her nipples. "Come for us, baby."

Keeping the toy in her channel, Sean bent down, capturing her clit between his lips.

She moaned and thrashed. "Yes. God. Yes."

Watching her orgasm gave him such joy. Her green eyes were glazed over with satisfaction. "You are so cute and adorable. I just want to eat you up."

She giggled.

He took the handcuffs off her wrists and rubbed them. "You did good, baby. Very good."

"I did, Sir?"

He kissed the woman who owned his heart. "Very."

* * * *

Jena's trembles continued as the two Doms she'd come to love continued training her. She'd used a vibrator before but never had it gotten her so hot so fast. It was more than the toy, which Sean used expertly on her pussy. It was both men, Matt and Sean, keeping her on edge, raising the pressure and need inside her. When she finally came, it had been earth shattering.

"Color?" Sean's demanding tone made her shivers intensify.

This was play, but it was also so powerful. "Green, Sir."

He crawled up her body until she felt the tip of his meaty cock on her pussy. "I'm going to fuck you, sub. I'm going to feel this pussy tighten around my cock. Do you understand?"

"Yes, Sir." *Please make love to me. Let me feel you inside my body. I must have you.* The pressure was returning with every tick of the clock, every beat of her heart, every dominant syllable from their mouths. She was on fire again and blazing hot.

He thrust his cock into her, piercing her pussy strongly. "You." His cock came out of her and she longed for its return. "Are." In again, deep and powerful. Then out again. "Mine." Another thrust, intense and complete. He continued the mantra, over and over, each thrust with a single word. "You. Are. Mine. You. Are. Mine."

Every nerve inside her was firing. Delicious dizziness overtook her. "Yes. God, yes. I'm yours, Master. I'm yours."

Sean's eyelids narrowed and he sent his cock deep into her pussy in a final plunge. Her womb clenched on his shaft again and again. She could feel his pulse inside her as he shot his seed into her body.

She fisted the sheets, feeling the orgasm throughout her entire being.

Sean rolled to the side and Matt took his place, filling her with his cock. His thrusts came even faster than Sean's, adding to the sensations already shooting through her body. She boiled from head to toe.

"Mine. Mine. Mine."

"Yes. Yes. Yes."

In no time, he came inside her. Again her pussy tightened, this time around her other man, her other Dom.

I am theirs. All of me.

Chapter Thirteen

Coming down from some of the best sex she'd ever had, Jena looked at the clock. "Oh my God. We're going to be late."

"Honey, don't worry. We've got time," Sean told her.

"We're only a block away, sweetheart," Matt said. "Besides, except for one meeting, our day is wide open."

"Meeting?" Scott's eyebrows shot up.

Matt pulled out his cell. "Just got a text from Erica that the Knights want to see all three of us at ten."

"I'm sure they want us to give them our plan of action to root out Lunceford's code."

"That's my guess. The meeting is at ten in the conference room on the third floor." Matt turned to her. "The official day starts at nine at TBK. So, we don't have to be there for another forty-five minutes."

"But I have to shower first, Sir."

Matt and Sean laughed.

"She's earned her stripes," Sean said. "Lesson is over, baby. You can call us by name now."

"All right, but I kind of like calling you Sirs and Masters. It fits."

"It might fit here, but not in public, baby." Matt left the bed. "Let's get you cleaned up."

"Seriously, I can do that on my own. Besides, you two might want to get something else started and we don't have the time."

Sean pinched her still-throbbing nipple. "If we want to start something, baby, we'll do it. That's not up to you."

"You tell her, bro." Matt sent her a wicked wink. "We can control ourselves, baby. Besides, I'd like to wash you."

"Knock yourself out, Masters, but please don't make me late. I'm still the new girl at TBK."

"You got it," Sean said, moving off the bed. "Come here, pet." He spread his arms wide, and she gazed at his muscled frame. Then she looked at Matt next to him, who was just as beautiful.

God, I'm one lucky girl.

She stood up and the men wrapped her in their arms, leading her to the shower.

* * * *

Jena walked into TBK Tower with Matt and Sean. "Hi, Terrence."

"Hello, Jena." The security guard smiled. "Hello, Mr. Dixon. Mr. MacCabe."

Sean waved. "Good morning."

"The big bosses in yet?" Matt asked.

"No, sir," Terrence answered. "Not sure they will be in, since their big day is tomorrow."

Jena had forgotten about Megan's wedding day. She still was stunned to be invited.

"I am sure they will be." Matt pulled out his phone. "I got a text from Erica that the Knights wanted to see us at ten."

As they all swiped their badges to enter the first secure area of the building, she took a deep breath, glancing around the room at all the people working. These were normal people, unlike her. She felt empty inside. Who was she kidding? The Knights might have put her on this job to weed out Lunceford's code, but they would never hire her permanently. Why would they? Her only career up until this point had been to hack and steal from companies. Hoping to ease her conscience, she'd always taken great care to pick the worst offenders in business—corporations so greedy they crushed their employees, polluted the environment, and moved money around the globe to keep from paying taxes. But that didn't change the fact that she was a hacker.

"Hello, guys," a nice-looking woman said, stepping next to them as they waited for the elevator.

"Anna, this is—"

"Robin Hood. I know." Anna smiled. "Everyone knows you, or at least your work. Your code has been keeping me up at nights for months. Glad you're not poking around the system anymore."

"Jena is on the team." Sean put his arm around her shoulder. "She's going to help us get Lunceford's code out."

"Very good," Anna said, extending her hand. "Nice to meet you, Jena."

"You, too." She shook the woman's hand.

As the doors opened to the elevator, Anna turned to her. "I would like to talk with you about some of your code."

"Sure. Happy to help." Jena wasn't sure what to make of the woman. Was she sincere or just putting up a front for Matt and Sean?

They all got on the elevator together.

"Anna, we have a meeting with the Knights at ten," Matt said. "We're open after that."

"Perfect." The woman swiped her card and punched the button for the second floor. "I'll assemble the rest of the techs. They are going to fall out of their chairs when they meet the real Robin Hood."

For a brief moment, Jena wondered if the woman was making digs at her. But just as fast, she shook it off. Destiny...Matt and Sean...Kimmie and her mom...her future—all of it she believed was worth whatever she had to do.

Jena smiled at the tech. "Anna, tell your buddies that Robin Hood is about to make her grand appearance."

* * * *

Jena watched the bride and grooms cut the cake. Megan looked stunning between her two husbands, Scott and Eric Knight. The love these three shared could be seen on their smiling faces and heard in their warm voices. The guys continued putting their arms around her, pulling her in tight. The kiss in the chapel had been the first that day but was definitely not the last.

The reception was being held at the hotel, which had a grand ballroom. The place looked like a fairy-tale castle. Every table had the finest crystal and china. White boxes with lavender ribbons were by each plate. Though she'd only known Megan for such a short time, it seemed so like the new bride to provide gifts to everyone. No two were the same, which stunned Jena even more. Megan was some kind of miracle worker.

Sean and Matt sat on either side of Jena. They'd opened their boxes. Sean's gift was a watch, and by the look of it, a very expensive watch, too. Matt's was a pair of boots that he was already trying on. She couldn't bring herself to open hers yet. Later. In private.

Megan held a bite of cake in each hand. She turned to the crowd. "Should I feed my husbands?" she asked with mischievousness in her eyes.

Everyone in the room roared their approval, including Jena.

Megan covered her guys' faces with cake. They both laughed and then each grabbed one of her wrists.

"Sweetheart, time to pay," Scott said, kissing her.

When he leaned back, Jena spotted a single glob of frosting on Megan's face. Eric held a bite of cake and so did Scott. They brought it to their bride's mouth, taunting her.

The crowd went wild. "Eat the cake. Make her pay," someone shouted, and everyone began to chant those words over and over.

Scott and Eric rubbed the bites on her lips. Jena knew they could've done more but was sure they were holding back not to embarrass their new wife too much. Megan might have to reapply lipstick, but the rest of her makeup remained flawless. God, the men in Destiny were so devoted to their women. Everywhere she looked, examples were right there in front of her. Ethel's men, Patrick and

Sam O'Leary, were doting on her like she was a virgin princess. How long had those three been together? Amber's guys, the Stone brothers, surrounded her like a bodyguard detail. Deputy Nicole could shoot the wings off of a butterfly, or so Jena had been told, but her guys, Erica's brothers, were glued to her every step. Erica, too, had the constant attention of Dylan and Cameron.

The celebration filled Jena with a warm feeling. Living in this community she believed would be so good for her, for Kimmie, and yes, even for her mom.

The band, Wolfe Mayhem, which was led by drummer Mitchell Wolfe, the sheriff's brother, fired up a song.

"Please welcome the new Knight family to the dance floor," Patrick O'Leary announced.

The crowd applauded as Scott and Eric led Megan to the center of the room. As they began to dance, Jena marveled at how fluidly they moved. She had no idea that two men and one woman could dance so beautifully together.

As the newlyweds enjoyed their first dance, Gretchen came up behind Jena, placing a hand on her shoulder. "My boys did good, didn't they?"

"Yes, they did." Jena turned around in her chair, grabbing the dear woman's hand. "They found their true love."

Gretchen wiped her eyes and nodded. "You haven't opened your gift yet, dear. Megan took great care picking out yours." Her voice was unusually hushed. "Open it."

Though Jena had wanted to wait, she couldn't refuse Gretchen. She opened the box and saw a necklace inside. It was a silver chain with a heart.

She smiled. "It's so lovely."

"Read the inscription," Gretchen said, her voice back to its strong British tone.

She flipped the heart around and felt her own eyes well up.

You are my sister of the heart. Love, Megan.

* * * *

Although it was Sunday, Jena was almost three hours into the workday. She sat back and stretched, looking at the screen which was flashing with more of Lunceford's malicious code. She'd isolated a big chunk of it that had been hidden in TBK's billing systems. Matt and Sean's praise had thrilled her. They weren't slouches either. With her assistance, their hands were flying over their keyboards, flushing out more of the viruses. It would take weeks, maybe months, to get all of TBK's systems cleaned out, but it would happen.

The door opened to her Texans' office and Megan walked in. "Jena, I need you to come with me."

"What for? What are you doing here? You got married yesterday," Sean said.

Megan smiled. "And now I'd like to have some girl talk and a very long lunch. It's a party. Don't expect me to bring Jena back until two."

"Lunch starts at noon, Megan," Matt teased. "And it's only supposed to be an hour. No more."

"Today it will be longer."

Sean grinned. "You're spoiling our employee."

"Jena is more than just an employee to you two bozos. I know it. Eric and Scott know it, too." Megan smiled. "Besides, whose last name is on this building?"

They laughed. "Yours," they said in unison.

"That's right. I want time alone with my friends. Jena happens to be one of them. The rest are on the top floor waiting."

Matt grinned. "The Fortress of Solace?"

"Whatever you want to call it. Yes."

"Dylan's most secure place on the planet has been invaded by women." Sean winked. "He's not going to like that."

"They are all trusted Destonians that have been cleared by Dylan for this party."

She smiled, feeling so very happy.

"What about our lunch?" Matt asked, making Jena smile. The man never forgot his stomach no matter what was going on.

"It's all arranged. Eric and Scott have a bunch of delicious food for you men."

"Sounds good to me," Sean said. "I could use a break."

"And I'm sure Jena could as well. You two work her too hard."

Yes, they do, but not here. In the bedroom, yes. But not too hard. Just right.

Matt came up to her and kissed her cheek. "Have fun, baby."

"Let's go," Megan said. "Everyone is waiting."

"Hold up." Sean grabbed Jena and gave her a quick kiss. "Don't stay away too long."

"I wouldn't dream of it, honey."

"Good grief." Megan rolled her eyes. "We're not going to Europe. We're only going upstairs. What are you two going to do when Jena comes with us on the shopping trip to Denver in two weeks?"

"We'll go with you," Matt informed.

"So like my two guys, Jena." Megan grinned. "The ladies of Destiny have tricks to keep our men on their toes. Come with me. You're about to learn some."

Sean grabbed her hand. "We'll walk you to the elevators."

"I expected as much," Megan said. "Dylan's changed your clearance. You have access to the top floor now."

Sean smiled. "You're kidding."

"It's true," her friend told him.

Matt slapped Sean on the back. "We're in the big league now, buddy."

"Listen to me, guys," Megan continued. "When we get to the top floor, you, Dylan, and my guys will have to leave."

She followed Megan to the elevators with Matt and Sean in tow. Megan swiped her card in the reader and then typed in a code on the console. The security for the top floor was even greater than the other floors.

The elevator doors opened and standing with their arms full of delicious smelling food were Eric and Scott Knight.

"Hey, guys." Sean stepped off the elevator.

"How are you coming along with the cleanup?" Eric asked.

Matt put his arm around Jena. "With this one on the team, much better."

Scott leaned down and kissed Megan. "Everyone is here, baby."

"You sure you're up for this, sweetheart?" Eric asked Megan.

"Don't be silly. Of course I'm up for this."

He kissed her. "Enjoy yourself. Once your party is over, we are taking you to see Doc Ryder for a thorough checkup."

"Fine." Megan grinned. "Now all you men must go. This floor is for women only for the next couple of hours."

* * * *

Sean looked around the conference table at the men who were having lunch with him. Scott and Eric had brought some delicious food from upstairs that the women of Destiny had prepared. The Knight brothers sat to his left. Across the table were Jason and Dylan. To his right was Matt, who was finishing off his second piece of Gretchen's homemade chocolate pie.

Dylan had brought Jason to this lunch so they could all get briefed on what was going on with the code.

"Did you leave any for us, Matt?" the sheriff asked with a grin.

"He better have," Scott said.

"You have no room to make that kind of demand on him." Sean jumped to Matt's defense. "You and Eric get to enjoy Gretchen's cooking all the time. We have to wait for the women to throw a party to taste her award-winning deserts."

"And that happens about every other week these days," Jason

said.

"I wonder what those women are up to in your office." Sean's mind was fixed on one particular party attendee, Jena, the love of his life.

Dylan shrugged. "Who knows?"

Sean looked at Scott and Eric. Both were grinning from ear to ear, which was a clue to what was really going on upstairs. "You guys know something, don't you?"

* * * *

Jena watched Megan stand up and face all the women. She was still wondering what this gathering was all about. She remembered hearing Scott talk about Doc Ryder. *Megan has got to be okay.*

"Ladies," Megan said, clicking her glass. "I know you must be wondering what this party is all about. Of course, we don't need much of a reason to throw a party, do we? But this time there is really something special I want to share with you."

Jena and the other women held their breaths.

"Don't leave them all hanging, young lady," Gretchen said. "Spill it."

Megan winked. "This is something special, Gretchen. Let me do this my way."

The woman smiled. "The floor is yours, my dear."

"You are my closest and dearest friends in Destiny," Megan told them.

Jena was shocked and thrilled that Megan had included her. She felt the same way for Megan and was beginning to feel that way for all the ladies.

"I wanted you to be the first to know," Megan continued. Her eyes welled up. "I wanted to show you my newest outfit."

Jena smiled. The woman's love of fashion had to be more than any other on the entire planet. Who threw a party for a new dress?

God, I love these people, but they are a little crazy.

Megan reached into a box and pulled out a maternity dress. "I'm going to be needing more of these."

Everyone gasped. Then Jena's heart soared for her new friend as everyone applauded and the combined chatter began.

"Oh my God."

"What wonderful news."

"Congratulations."

"Do you know if it's a boy or girl?"

"What did your men say?"

Gretchen quieted the excited group. "Get your glasses, ladies. Here's the champagne. Megan, I brought you some apple cider. So good for the baby."

When everyone's glass was filled, Ethel stood to give a toast to the new mother-to-be. "Megan, you have made all of us feel so very special in your life today by sharing this wonderful news. I am sure I speak for all of us when I say that we love you, Eric, and Scott so very much. You supported our community by giving of yourself. And now you are blessing us with a new little baby that I know you will allow us to spoil. I can see all of us fighting over the little one now."

"I'll win that fight, Ethel," Gretchen said, wiping her eyes.

"We all will," Ethel said sweetly. "The important thing is, we are all here for you, Megan. And when you are tired, overwhelmed, and need any of us, we will come running. But always know that anything you go through is worth it all. Take it from a judge—you will be a wonderful mother. We love you."

Everyone applauded and drank their champagne through the happy tears.

* * * *

Sean restated his question to Scott and Eric. "What is going on upstairs, guys? You do know."

"You're damn right we do," Scott said.

Eric nodded. "Megan is going to have a baby. We're going to be dads."

They all stood up with their cans of soda and made a toast to the two lucky men. Sean imagined a day when he and Matt would be announcing Jena's pregnancy. The truth was, when they brought Kimmie back to Destiny, he would be a new dad. He could already feel it in his heart. He couldn't wait to have Jena, her mom, and little Kimmie living in his and Matt's house. They would make it a home.

"You lucky dog." Sean slapped Eric on the back. "Megan said we would get Jena back by two, but now that I know what the party is really about I'm sure we won't see her until five."

"You're right about that," the father-to-be answered.

The intercom buzzed.

Scott clicked the button. "Yes?"

"Mr. Knight. This is Terrence at the front desk. I have Sheriff Wolfe's brothers here saying they need to see him with an urgent matter."

"Send them up," Scott said.

"Do you need us to leave?" Matt asked Jason.

"I have no idea what this is about, so no. Stay." The sheriff seemed perplexed.

There was always tension surrounding the trio. Anyone near them when they were together sensed it. Jason was the oldest of the three, followed by Lucas and then Mitchell. Lucas was a successful architect. Mitchell was a drummer, songwriter, dreamer, and a well-known hothead.

The doors opened. The two younger Wolfe brothers rushed straight to Jason.

"Why didn't you tell us about Phoebe?" Mitchell's face was red hot.

"About Phoebe? What?" Jason asked.

"The calls. From the guy," Lucas shot back at the sheriff. "How many times has she been contacted by him?"

"Calm down, guys," Dylan said. "My cousin is going to be fine. I'm helping your brother on this one."

"I've got this," Jason told them. "Phoebe thinks whoever is making these calls is harmless."

"That's not what Shannon thinks," Lucas snapped back.

"It appears that I need to talk to Shannon about confidentiality again. I'm the sheriff. Leave this to me."

"Good God, Jason. You're our brother." Mitchell leaned forward. "We're still concerned about Phoebe's well-being. So are you. Don't leave us in the dark."

"I'm handling it."

Lucas glared at him. "Just like you did the last time. We all know how that ended."

Sean could see the pain in all three of the Wolfe brothers' faces. They'd lost Phoebe. He couldn't imagine what it would feel like to lose Jena.

"Whatever is going on is police business," Jason said firmly.

"I guess we'll handle this ourselves." Mitchell turned and stormed out of the room.

Lucas stared at Jason, appearing to want to say more. But the man didn't. Instead, he bolted out after Mitchell.

"Excuse me, fellows." Jason went after his brothers.

"What the hell?" Matt asked, mirroring Sean's own sentiments.

"First I've heard about the phone calls, but apparently we all need to be concerned for Phoebe." Scott pushed his empty plate away, turning to Dylan. "I hope you and Jason fill us in if you get any news about this caller."

"We will," he said.

"Speaking of getting filled in." Scott turned to Sean and Matt. "Get us up to speed on what you've found on Kip's code."

Sean liked both the Knights. They were incredibly astute businessmen.

"Looks like we'll need another few months, but the bulk of it should be out of the system in a couple weeks."

Dylan's cell went off. "It's Black." He brought it up to his ear. "Strange here."

Dylan nodded. "Good to hear. Yes. We will. They are here with me. Got it. I'll tell them. See you tomorrow." He clicked it off and turned to him and Matt. "The missing laptop has popped up again."

Black had almost had the goods on Niklaus Mitrofanov last month, connecting him to a shill company involved in the ransom money sent by the Knights for Erica. The agent who found the information died before he could get the laptop with the data in the right hands.

"Where is it?" Matt asked.

"In transit," Dylan answered. "We have to keep this under wraps until it's stateside."

"How? I thought Redding had the laptop and was dead." Sean wanted that laptop at TBK as soon as possible.

"Grayson is a better agent than either Black or I thought. The body that was found wasn't his. It was a decoy. Gave him time to slip out of the country. He's in Hong Kong right now, on his way back. Black is coming here tomorrow. Grayson should be here next week."

"Damn, that's fucking good news," Matt said.

"There's more," Dylan turned to Scott and Eric. "Lunceford is being moved to another facility. Black called in some favors. The bastard will be residing at ADX Florence."

Sean was happy about that. Kip would finally be in a cage that his digital claws couldn't escape.

"And what is this ADX place?" Scott asked.

"It's the Alcatraz of the Rockies," Matt answered. "It houses male inmates in the federal prison system deemed the most dangerous and in need of the tightest control. No place on the planet is more locked down than it."

Sean turned to Dylan. "When?"

"Next week they transfer Lunceford. There's more for you two," Dylan told him and Matt. "The team Black put on tracking down Braxton got a lead. They're fairly certain he's in Chicago. Two of his best agents are there now and checking into it."

"God, this is good news." Tomorrow, he, Jena, and Matt would head to Albuquerque to get her daughter and mother and bring them back to Destiny. "Kip is shoved in a box he can't get out of. The evidence we need to get Mitrofanov put away for good is on its way to Destiny. Carl Braxton is on the run. And Scott and Eric are going to be dads."

"Finally, things are going our way," Matt said.

"You can say that again, bro."

For the first time in a long time, he felt like the good guys were finally tipping the balance. Jena was here, safe.

* * * *

Jena sat between Nicole and Phoebe. The champagne was flowing generously, pulling out giggles and silliness from all the women present. She felt nice and warm herself. What a place Destiny was. Everyone supported each other.

Amber and her sister, Belle, were laughing at a private joke.

"You better share it with the rest of us," Nicole piped up. "Or I might have to arrest you."

"I was just telling Belle that I'm going to feel really good with my guys at Phase Four tonight." Amber smiled. "If you give me another drink, I might even make it up to the main stage."

More laughter erupted.

Jena looked at the group. "This is new to me. What can you tell me about Phase Four? And more importantly—BDSM?"

Amber looked at Jena and smiled. "I'll tell you one thing. It's the most fun I've ever had in my life."

"Hear, hear." The group raised their glasses.

"Now, ladies, I totally agree with you, but this young woman has asked us a serious question." Ethel stepped in front of her. "Jena, I've been in the life since I married my two amazing men. Yes, it's fun, but it is also about deepening the relationship. Like most of the ladies will agree, the first time you enter Phase Four you are nervous. No matter how much you've been told, you still aren't sure what to expect. But you go because you're so in love with your men. You soon learn it's about trust. But what you learn the most is how very much your men love you. They deliver the highest expression of love by making you the center of their very existence. It's all about you."

"Tell her about the paddlings, Ethel." Amber sat down in her chair in a fit of laughter.

"Sweetheart," the grand lady said to her. "You will discover more about yourself than you can imagine. There are no rules except the ones you and your Doms give each other. The club is a place for those of us in the life to celebrate our love publically. Not everyone takes the stage. Some of us, me included, keep most of our play private. Others enjoy the freedom of Phase Four. All of us support each other. None of us condemns what happens between people in love." Ethel paused. "I'm rambling, aren't I?" she asked, looking at her half-empty glass.

"Yes, you are," Gretchen said. "That's how you Irish folks answer a simple question."

"I'm not Irish and you know it."

"You married two of them, Ethel. That makes you Irish in my book." Gretchen turned to Jena. "One thing my dear friend left out was those of us who haven't found our true loves, like me. I love my life taking care of Megan and her two wonderful guys. There has been no room for a man in my life, but that doesn't mean I'm dead. I enjoy the pleasure a man can give me from time to time. Quit grinning, Megan."

"Sorry, Gretchen. You know I love you."

"So understand, Jena, BDSM has a place for all kinds—those in love, those looking for love, and those of us looking for a good time."

"I always knew you were a trollop, Gretchen," Ethel teased.

"No argument from me, you Irish tart."

The room fell apart from hysterical laughter and so did Jena. She had never felt more at home anywhere in all her life.

Chapter Fourteen

At Sheriff Wolfe's office, Matt sat on one side of Jena and Sean sat on the other. Dylan and Black stood by the window. Jason was behind his desk.

"The laptop should be here next week," Black told them. "It will have all you need to arrest Mitrofanov."

"That's what I'm hoping for, but you've told us that before." Jason stared at the man. "I hope you don't let us down this time."

"I won't," Black said behind his mirrored sunglasses.

Dylan was wearing his own pair. "Any word on where Niklaus is? We haven't seen him in Destiny since he left for his nephews' funerals in Chicago."

"He's back," Jason said. "Mitchell saw him and his crew going into his house twenty minutes ago. My brother lives two doors down from Mitrofanov's house."

Matt tensed. "It's time to get Jena out of town then."

"We've been planning on going to get her daughter and mother," Sean added. "No time like the present."

From the other side of the door, Shannon's voice could be heard. "You can't go in there, Mr. Mitrofanov."

The door swung open and in walked the fat, bald-headed slug holding a file. "I'm glad we are all here, especially this one." He pointed his crooked finger at Jena.

Pulling out their guns, he and Sean jumped to their feet in front of the mobster, keeping her safely behind them.

Out of the corner of his eyes, Matt could see Dylan, Black, and Jason had their weapons in hand, too.

"Gentlemen, please. I am unarmed and alone. I came here as a concerned citizen. Very concerned. Without a cat, mice feel free. It's an old Russian saying, but appropriate now. Lower your weapons."

"Everyone, put away your guns," Jason said through clenched teeth. "I'll keep mine in my hand just in case Mr. Mitrofanov makes any sudden moves."

"Now, isn't that much better, gentlemen?"

Matt glared at the kingpin. "Whatever you came to say, now's the time."

"This woman is a thief, Sheriff Wolfe." Niklaus placed his file on the desk. "See for yourself."

"That's rich, Mitrofanov," Sean said. "You, of all people, accusing her of stealing. You're a fucking liar."

"Cool it, MacCabe. Let me see what's in here." Jason opened the file and began reading.

Matt's pulse was racing. He had the training to slice the fucker's throat in a split second without getting a drop of blood on his clothes.

Why not? Jena wouldn't have to face the monster ever again.

He knew why not. Patience had to be practiced here, no matter how much Mitrofanov tried to goad them. The bastard would end up in prison or in a grave soon enough. Jena would remain safe. He would see to that.

Jason looked up from the file. "What do you expect me to do with this, Mitrofanov?"

"I expect you to arrest this woman for stealing. I lost ten grand because of her."

"You lost ten grand because of a hacker by the name of Robin Hood. What proof do you have that she is that person?"

"Proof? Everyone here knows she's Robin Hood. I don't need any more proof than that."

"But you do. It's the law. I can't arrest her on this pile of shit."

Mitrofanov grabbed up the file and spun around. "Miss?"

"Not one fucking step closer, asshole," Matt told him.

"Of course, but I want to hear it from the lady's own mouth if she is or is not the Robin Hood hacker."

"Get out of my office," Jason ordered the mobster. "I'm the only one allowed to interrogate here. Not you."

"This isn't over, Sheriff. You will be hearing from my attorney." The fucker stormed out of the office and slammed the door behind him.

"We need the laptop, Black," Jason said.

"You'll get it." The man turned to him and Sean. "Time for you two to get Jena and go dark."

* * * *

Pulling out her cell, Jena watched Matt and Sean pack their bags. Her suitcase was ready. She still couldn't believe that she was running again. Thankfully, this time she wasn't alone.

Jena punched her mother's number into the phone for the third time, hoping it didn't go to voicemail again. She was starting to get concerned.

This isn't like my mom at all. "We can take turns driving. I don't want to stop."

Ring. Ring. Ring. *Please answer.* Ring. Ring. Ring.

A cold chill ran through her body as the voicemail picked up. Her heart raced.

"Baby, still no word from your mom?" Matt asked.

"No. I'm getting worried," she confessed.

Sean's phone went off and she jumped. "This is MacCabe. Fuck. Yes. We'll head straight to the airport. Got it. Thanks." He turned to her and Matt. "That was Dylan. Black got word that Braxton left Chicago yesterday."

"Oh my God." Her hands were shaking. The monster was out and on the move.

Sean wrapped his arms around her. "Dylan is going to have the

Knights' private jet ready to take us to Kimmie. No fifteen-hour drive."

"I've got to get to my baby."

* * * *

Jena was in total panic. The drive to the airport had taken forty minutes and she'd tried several times to reach her mother. Still no answer.

She ran to the plane. A man stood beside the jet waving them forward.

"That's Joshua Phong," Sean told her, running beside her.

Matt was on her other side. "He's the Knights' pilot."

They boarded the plane, and she turned to Joshua. "Please hurry."

"I will go as fast as this plane can go. And that's fast. We should be landing in Albuquerque in about an hour." Joshua went to the cockpit.

She and her guys sat down and buckled in. Her heart thudded in her chest. "Carl can't get to my baby before I do."

Sean grabbed her hand. "Honey, just because he left Chicago doesn't mean he knows where Kimmie and your mom are. He could be anywhere."

"And remember, Dylan and Black are on the horn with operatives in New Mexico," Matt said. "They should be at your mom's place soon. Just hold on, baby. Hold on."

"I'm trying," she told them. "But this is the hardest thing I've ever faced."

"We're with you." Sean squeezed her fingers gently. "Everything is going to be okay."

Like Joshua had told them, they landed a little over an hour later. A car was waiting for them. Sean and Matt threw their luggage in the trunk.

She grabbed her phone and was about to dial her mom when it

rang. Hope swelled inside her. Only one person had this number. "Mom, are you and Kimmie okay?"

"Hi, Jena." A voice that filled her with dread came through the speaker. "It's been a long time."

How had Kip Lunceford gotten this number? She should've ditched the burner phone a long time ago. She didn't have time for this. "What do you want?"

"Just letting you know that your Kimmie is safe for now."

Her heart jumped up into her throat. "If you did anything to my baby or my mom I swear—"

"Don't, Jena. You have no power here. I do, and I've always found a father's love for his little girl to be special."

Her blood turned to ice in her veins. "I will kill you!" she screamed.

The connection was lost.

Matt grabbed the phone from her, and Sean pulled her into his body.

"What, baby?" Matt asked.

"That was Kip. He sent Carl to my house to get Kimmie."

Without a word, they got in the car. Sean hit the gas.

Please, God, please. Let me get to my baby before he does. Let her be safe.

* * * *

With her heart pounding faster than ever before, Jena rushed into the tiny rental house. Matt and Sean had their guns drawn, as did she. *Please, God. Please.* "Kimmie! Mom!"

Seeing the shambles the living space was in filled her with dread.

She peered into the tiny kitchen. Nothing.

Shaking, she went down the hall to Kimmie's room.

Her daughter wasn't there. The pit of her stomach twisted into a sick knot.

Please, God.

She moved to her mother's room with Matt and Sean. Empty.

Losing hope, she went to the bathroom, the only place left in the house.

The door was shut.

She opened it and saw her mother on the floor bleeding. Her eyes were closed.

She fell to the ground. "Mom?"

Her mother moaned.

She's alive. "Call 9-1-1."

Matt grabbed his phone, but before he could call they all heard sirens in the background.

She turned back to her mother and saw her cell in her hand. "Mom? Talk to me."

Her mother's eyes fluttered but didn't open.

"Please, Mom. You have to tell me where Kimmie is. Please. She has to be safe."

Her mom's lips vibrated slightly.

She leaned down closer. "Mom, wake up. Please. Help me."

As the sirens got louder, one word was all she could hear from her mother.

"Carl."

Chapter Fifteen

Sean stood beside Jena, who was holding her mother's hand.

She needed him to remain calm and in control, which, thanks to his training, he was able to achieve. He'd already sent a text to Dylan about what they'd found. Where were the agents that were supposed to have come here earlier?

He glanced over at Matt, who was giving his statement to the police.

The EMTs placed Jena's mother on the gurney. He could see where some of Jena's strength had come from. There was blood and skin under her fingernails. She'd apparently gotten in a good swipe on Braxton before he punched her in the face several times.

Jena hadn't stopped trembling, but she had stopped talking after her mother uttered Braxton's name.

He'd seen that same look before. Jena's face reminded him of his battlefield days. Too many times he'd seen the same gaze on his fellow soldiers. Blank. Absent. He knew she was in a total state of shock. No wonder. Her mother was injured and they had no idea where Braxton had taken Kimmie. No clue at all.

Fuck.

Two men walked into the rental house. It was plain to see by their demeanor and clothing they were from the Agency.

Too late, buddies. Fuck.

They presented identifications to the officer in charge.

Matt finished giving his statement to the policeman and walked back to Jena and Sean. One of the agents continued talking to the sergeant, and the other headed straight to them.

Sean moved a few steps from Jena, fearing what he might learn from the man. She didn't need to hear the worst.

The agent stood in front of him and Matt. "Dixon?"

"That's me," Matt answered.

"I'm MacCabe."

"White," the man told them.

"Why so late, White?" he asked him, unable to hold back the rage in his tone.

White removed his sunglasses. "Black thinks it was Lunceford."

"Lunceford what?"

"My partner got a call from someone posing as an Agency analyst that said Braxton was spotted in Roswell with a little girl. We headed that way immediately. Once we got ahold of Black to tell him the change, he blew his top saying that it had to be Kip Lunceford's doing."

Sean knew how brilliant the psycho could be. Breaking into an agent's phone was child's play to Lunceford. This was all a game to the fucker, and right now, Kip was winning.

"Black ordered us back here to report to you," White continued.

Sean's appreciation for Black grew. He was putting them in the driver's seat.

The EMTs took Jena's mom out the front door.

Jena stepped up beside him, determination back in her green eyes. She glared at White. "Where is my child?" She must've been listening while they were talking.

White's phone rang. He looked at the screen. "This is from our team. White here. Yes. You are? The line went dead." The agent turned to him. "That was another tip that Braxton is in a motel on the outskirts of the city." He handed the phone to Matt, who took down the address. "Don't get your hopes up, miss. It might be Lunceford again."

"It's all we have to go on. Even if it is Kip pulling the strings, I have to go." Jena turned to him and Matt. "I've got to find Kimmie right now. I'll just have to check on my mom later."

Sean put his arm around her. "Your mom is tough. She'll be okay."

White motioned to his partner. "We've got this here. Go."

As they ran out the door, Sean did something he hadn't done since standing next to Matt and watching the flames of the compound take his parents' lives. He prayed.

* * * *

Jena looked at the flea trap motel the anonymous caller had sent them to. "There it is."

"I'm going to park across the street so he doesn't see us," Sean said.

My baby's got to be okay. Please, God, let her be okay.

"Room seven," Matt reminded them. "There looks to be about ten rooms in the entire place. If you park in front of that truck, we'll have the best view."

As Sean stopped the car, she saw Carl come out of a room with a cigarette in his hand. "Oh my God."

She didn't hesitate, jumping out of the car, pulling out her gun, and running to the man who had her baby.

From behind, she could hear Matt and Sean calling her name.

It didn't matter.

Kimmie needed her.

She couldn't stop for them or for anyone.

She had to save her baby, had to hold her again. "Where's Kimmie, you bastard?"

Carl rushed her.

She fired, but he kept coming.

Before she could get another round off, he grabbed her, twisting the gun out of her hand. "You hit me, bitch."

"Let her go, Braxton." Matt aimed his pistol at the fucker.

Jena couldn't see Sean. Where was he?

Carl squeezed her against his chest, keeping his body behind hers. He held the gun to her head. "Put down your weapon, asshole, or she dies."

Matt didn't. "Let's all calm down. We only want to make sure Kimmie is okay. You can understand that, can't you?" *He's stalling. Sean must be moving quietly to get Carl.*

"I understand more than you know. This cunt ruined my life—she and her goddamn family. Put down your gun now or I'll blow her brains out. You'd like to join your daddy, wouldn't you, Jena?"

Fuming, she lifted her leg and slammed her heel into his toes and shoved her elbow into his stomach.

Carl's grip loosened.

A gun fired from their left.

She turned around and saw the fucker fall to the sidewalk, blood pouring out of his head.

She bolted to room seven. "Kimmie?"

"Mommy?"

She lifted her little girl into her arms, kissing her face through tears of relief. "I'm here, baby. Mommy is here."

Chapter Sixteen

Jena held her mother's fingers. It was so hard to see her in a hospital bed with an IV and an oxygen tube in her nose. Sean was in the recliner with a sleeping Kimmie in his arms. Matt had gone to get coffee.

Her two guys had won her daughter over quickly, reminding her about her birthday. Jena knew it had only been a way to distract her from what had been going on outside the motel room, but it had worked to put a smile on Kimmie's face. Being five years old had some advantages.

God, she loved Matt and Sean. They'd made sure that Kimmie didn't come out of the motel room until Carl's body was removed.

What a night. Carl was no longer a threat to her and Kimmie. He was dead. Her mother's condition was stable. It was clear to everyone on the scene that her mom had put up quite the fight. The fucker had broken her mother's nose and both her wrists, but the worst of the lot was the knife wound in her stomach. She'd been rushed into surgery to repair the damage. The procedure was a success.

The surgeon entered the room, which pleased Jena. It was late, but the doctor wasn't rushing. He had her mom's chart in his hand. He looked at the monitor and took a couple of notes.

"How's she doing?" she asked.

"I wish all my patients were as tough as Janet Taylor." The surgeon turned to her. "I was a big fan of your dad."

"Me, too. I sure miss him." She glanced over at Kimmie in Sean's arms, reminding her how wonderful it had been when her own dad was still alive.

"I'm going to keep your mom sedated for the night just so she can rest. Tomorrow morning we will get her up on her feet and walking the halls."

"I don't think that is going to be a problem for Mom."

The doctor chuckled. "I'm sure it won't be. If you have any issues, get the nurse to page me. I'm pretty sure tonight will be nice and quiet for your mom."

"Thank you, Doctor."

The surgeon left.

"Honey, you want to take this chair and get some sleep?" Sean asked quietly.

"No. I couldn't sleep. Not now." She had a lot to think about. *How am I going to tell Mom about Matt and Sean?* She wasn't sure how her mom would take the news that she was in love with two men and they were in love with her. Her mother was more than just a parent to her. She was her friend. This news might shock her mom, but she deserved to know how happy Matt and Sean had made her daughter.

Matt returned with the coffee, quietly shutting the door. "Here you go, baby."

She took the cup. "Thanks, honey."

He kissed her and then walked over to Kimmie and Sean. "How's our little trooper?"

"She's amazing and sound asleep," Sean told him.

Her heart was theirs. Somehow, she would find just the right words to tell her mother everything. She prayed her mom would understand.

"I love you, Mom," she whispered again.

* * * *

As the early morning sun filtered in through the windows of the hospital room, Jena saw her mom's eyes open and a weak smile appeared on her face. "Mom, oh, Mom, I was so worried about you."

"Don't waste your time on fretting, sweetheart, your mom is a lot stronger than you think. I'm just a little roughed up, but you should see the other guy." Her mom giggled.

Jena could tell her mother was still coming out of the morphine the doctor had given her for pain. "Always with the jokes. I love you, Mom."

"I love you, too, my wonderful daughter. How in the world did you get here so fast and how did you know I was in trouble?" Her mom's eyes widened. "Oh my God, where is Kimmie?"

"I'm right here, Grandma."

"Oh, my sweet angel, come here and give Grandma a big kiss."

"What in the world is this contraption, Jena?" She pushed the morphine pump.

"That's your pain medication, Mom."

"Oh my God, I just pushed it."

"It's okay. It won't give it to you unless it's time for another dose."

"I don't need it. I'm perfectly fine."

"That's because you used it during the night to keep you comfortable."

"You mean I used it?"

"Yes. I know you probably don't remember it, but you did." Jena squeezed her mother's hand. "Everything is fine and wonderful, Mom, but I need to fill you in and there is something very important I've got to tell you."

Matt came in with the coffee and saw Jena's mom awake and looking much better. "Hi, Mrs. Taylor. I'm Matt. I guess you've already met Sean?"

"Not exactly, young man, but I did notice him holding my granddaughter. As good looking as you both are, if I hadn't seen Kimmie and Jena, I would have thought I'd died and gone to heaven."

They all laughed. Jena could see the result of that last pump of morphine on her mother's face.

"Hey, Sean, why don't we take Kimmie to the cafeteria and see if they have ice cream?"

"Sounds like a good idea to me. What do think, Kimmie?"

"Yes, sir, I like ice cream."

"Then let's go so we can give your mom and grandma time to catch up."

Jena was so proud of her men. They had already started bonding with Kimmie. You could see it on their faces. *What amazing dads they will be.*

Jena watched as the door closed behind them. "Mom, I'm so glad you're better. It's going to take time to heal and I'm sure you'll need therapy on those wrists, but, before long you'll be good as new."

"Now, Jena, I think it's time for you to tell me everything that transpired since you found me. You were the one to find me, right?"

Jena told her mom every single detail of the past events, including Carl's demise. Her mother thought it was sad that Carl never learned his lesson before it was too late, but was very glad they didn't have to be worried anymore.

"Now, young lady, what is this important news you want to tell me? I have a feeling it has something to do with those two good-looking men I just met."

"You are so observant, aren't you?"

"I may have black eyes, but I can see very well how you look at each other. Now fill me in on all the exciting details."

"Mom, exciting?"

"Yes, dear, get on with it."

She took a deep breath. "Please don't be shocked about what I'm going to tell you."

"Oh, Jena, for goodness sake, you love them both. Now please tell me the rest."

"Mom, you never cease to amaze me."

"I know they love you. It's written all over their faces. So, where do we go from here?"

Jena told her Mom about her wonderful guys, about Destiny, and about all the friendly, quirky people there. She also told her about the common practice of polygamy.

"Jena, there have been two times in my life that I've been this happy. The first was when I married your dad and the second was when that good-looking race car driver and I had you. You tell me about this great town with its crazy, fun-loving residents and that we get to move there. I can't tell you how happy you've made me. I will have two great sons-in-law that want me, too."

"We're not married yet, Mom."

"That's just a formality, dear."

Matt, Sean, and Kimmie walked back into the room singing "The Farmer in the Dale."

Jena thought they looked so cute together.

A big grin covered her mother's face. "Come here, young men, and give your new mom a big hug and kiss."

"Mom." Jena was quite shocked at her mother's forwardness.

"Jena," Sean said, "I think she is absolutely wonderful." He walked to the bed and gave her mom a huge hug and a kiss on the cheek.

"I love her," Matt chimed in and he, too, gave her a big hug and kiss.

"These boys are brilliant," her mom said. "They picked the most beautiful girl in the world."

* * * *

"Mommy," Kimmie pleaded as she tugged on Jena's pants, "I need to go potty."

"Sure, sweet girl," Jena said. "Guys, will you take care of Mom while I take Kimmie to the restroom? We need a little time together anyway, so I'm going to the park across the street where we can have some mother and daughter time." She winked at her men.

"Of course," Sean said. "My pleasure. Have a good time together."

"That will give us time to visit with your...I mean our mom." Matt turned to Kimmie. "Be good for Mommy and take care of her. Make sure she looks both ways before crossing the street."

"I will, Mr. Matt." Kimmie grabbed Jena's hand. "See, I'm being real good."

"Yes, you are," Sean said, smiling.

"I'm very proud of you," Matt chimed in.

"Mommy," Kimmie whispered, "Mr. Matt said he was proud of me."

"I heard," Jena whispered back. "Bye, guys, bye, Grandma. We will be back shortly."

* * * *

Matt watched Jena and Kimmie leave the hospital room.

Sean turned to him. "I'll follow them to make sure they are safe, but will stay back far enough so they can have their time together."

"Great thinking, bro. That way I can take care of Mom in case she needs anything."

Janet's eyes widened. "I thought you said Carl was dead?"

"He is, but there is more you need to know," Matt said.

"I'm out of here," Sean said. "Best to stay as close as possible."

"Go on," Janet pleaded. "I want to know absolutely every last detail."

Matt clued Janet in on all that had been going on, with assurance that he and Sean would make sure they would all be safe.

"I'm so proud of my girl for picking two wonderful men to share her life with."

"Actually, Mom, She didn't have a choice. Sean and I fell madly in love with her. She's our world and now, and you and Kimmie are, too."

* * * *

Jena sat on the swings with Kimmie.

"Mommy, can we sing 'The Farmer in the Dale' like I did with Mr. Sean and Mr. Matt?"

"Sure, honey, let's pretend we are very sad when we sing it."

They both acted like they were crying and then they sang it happy and finally angry.

Jena was so happy being with her little girl again and having so much fun together.

"Mr. Matt and Mr. Sean are so funny, Mommy. Mr. Sean sounds just like all my favorite cartoon characters and Mr. Matt knows magic. He pulled a quarter out of my ear. I really, really, really like them, Mommy. In fact, I like them to the moon."

"Mommy really, really, really likes them, too. In fact, sweetheart, Mommy loves them."

"Like you love me?"

"Yes, like I love you—to the moon and back."

"Okay, Mommy, then I love them, too—to the moon and back."

"Kimmie, I have a very big, important question to ask you."

"This big?" Kimmie stretched her arms wide.

"Yes, sweetheart, that big, and I want you to think very carefully about your answer, okay?"

"Sure, I will."

"How would you like to move to Colorado with Mr. Matt and Mr. Sean?"

"What's a Colorado?"

"It's another state. You were living in New Mexico, which is a state."

"What about Grandma?"

"She'll go, too."

"We all love each other, right?"

"Yes, honey."

"Then I say yes, yes, yes."

"You've made me very happy, Kimmie, so I think a big birthday party will be in store for you in our new home with Mr. Sean and Mr. Matt."

Chapter Seventeen

Three days later, Sean carried a big box from the trunk to the house. "Last one, sweetheart."

Jena held out an ice-cold beer for him. "You tired?"

"No. I'm good." She, Kimmie, and her mom had been on the run from Carl for so long, the three didn't have many personal possessions. *That's going to change. I'm going to give them the world.* He set the box down on the floor and took a sip of the beer. "Where's Mom?"

"She's watching television in her room." Jena kissed him. "She loves it here. Kimmie does, too."

"Where is the birthday girl?"

They'd had a small party for Kimmie in the hospital room on her actual birthday, but now they were going to celebrate it Destiny style.

"Matt took her out on the porch. They're playing tea party." Jena grabbed his hand. "I have something I need to talk to you about."

The seriousness in her tone got his attention instantly. "I'm listening, baby."

"Kimmie came to me this morning and crawled into bed with me. You and Matt were making breakfast. She told me she loved you and Matt so very much. After a few kisses and cuddles, Kimmie asked me if I would be okay if she called Mr. Matt and Mr. Sean 'daddy.'" Jena's eyes widened. "Would you be okay with that?"

"Okay? I am thrilled she wants to. God, I never dreamed I would have this kind of life." He laughed. *A perfect life filled with joy, laughter, and love.* He pulled Jena close, kissing her.

Without a word, he headed out the back door with Jena to Kimmie and Matt and swept his daughter into his arms. "Matt, do you know what this sweet girl told her mommy this morning?"

"What?"

"She wants to call both of us 'daddy.'"

Matt stood and took Kimmie, giving her his own hug. "Little one, you've just made me and Daddy Sean the happiest men in the world."

Jena came up beside Sean and put her arm around his waist. "We're a real family now."

"Yes, we are, sweetheart. Now and forever." After a little more invisible tea for all of them, Sean turned to Jena and Matt. "We need to head to the Knight's place in a couple of hours."

"I can't believe Megan is doing this for us." She winked, keeping the secret from Kimmie.

Jena didn't know the half of it. She thought that Megan was throwing an impromptu birthday party for their daughter. She expected a small gathering, but one thing about Destonians that Sean had come to learn was they loved a party, and especially over-the-top ones. The whole town was likely to be at Kimmie's birthday party.

When they came back into the house, Matt took Kimmie to her room to pick out an outfit. Earlier, their little princess had already taken Sean to see her choices for the day, which had only been narrowed down to five at the time. He grinned, hoping Matt would have better luck getting her to choose one.

He and Jena went to see how they could help Mom get ready.

She was sitting on the bed, holding a mirror, staring at her reflection. "Oh, Jena, how can I meet your new friends looking like this?"

"A little makeup will work magic," Jena told her mother.

"Mom, everyone here will understand what you've been through." Sean held the hand of the wonderful woman. "You'll find the people of this town are not judgmental in any way."

She set down the mirror and held up her arms, each having its own splint. "I know I have to go. I'm just embarrassed. My face looks like a big fat ape's."

He leaned down and kissed her on the cheek. "Not a chance, Mom. You're a nice-looking woman. Besides, you'll soon forget your injuries because you'll be having so much fun."

"Sean, thank you for everything you've done for Jena and Kimmie…and for me. You and Matt are the best sons a woman could ever hope for."

Kimmie ran in with the pink dress on that he'd liked best of all.

He patted Matt on the back. "Good job, buddy."

"She knew you liked it best and asked me if I did, too. So, good job for both of us."

"Mommy, will you fix my hair pretty to meet your new friend, Mrs. Knight?"

"Yes, baby." Jena turned to her mother. "Mom, I'll be back to help you get ready."

"Young lady, I'm not helpless. I can put my own makeup on." Mom giggled. "Please tell me you have a quart of foundation. It's going to take that much for me to paint this old barn."

* * * *

Jena stood behind Kimmie and her mom as they walked into the Knight Mansion. Megan greeted them and gave a special hug to her mom. "I'm so glad to meet you, Mrs. Taylor."

"Nice to meet you. Please, call me Janet."

"I will. Call me Megan." She knelt down. "You must be the little girl I've been hearing so much about."

"My name is Kimmie," her daughter answered, holding her tiny hand out like she'd been taught.

Megan shook her hand. "May I have a hug, too?"

Kimmie nodded, wrapping her arms around her friend.

Jena looked over at her mom, whose eyes were wide, taking in the beauty of the room.

"Megan, your home is lovely," her mother said. "I've never seen anything like it in my life."

"Wait until you see the rest of it," Matt said. "This is only the foyer. It gets better."

"Much," Sean added.

"Stop it." Megan shook her head. "It is something. I never dreamed I would be living in such a place."

"Your guys want to give you the best," Jena said. "You're worth it."

"I would be happy anywhere with them, but it is nice to have this home to share with family and friends. And speaking of that, I want to take Kimmie to the ballroom. I think she's going to like what's in there."

Megan took Kimmie by the hand and led them down the hallway.

When they arrived at the large room, the crowd, which Jena hadn't been expecting, cheered. "Happy birthday, Kimmie," they shouted.

Her daughter jumped up and down. "Is that my birthday cake?" She pointed to the giant dessert on the table. It was decorated with princes and princesses and little fairies.

"Yes, it is," Megan answered. "Since you are the little princess, you need to wear this tiara." She placed it on Kimmie's head.

The entire ballroom was decked out like a fairy-tale wonderland. How in the world had Megan pulled this together?

"This is my party, Mommy? This is for me?"

"Yes, it is. All for you." She kissed her daughter on the cheek, thrilled beyond words that her friend had done this. "Say 'thank you' to Mrs. Knight."

"Thank you, Mrs. Knight. I am five years old now. I'm a big girl."

"Yes, you are. You're very welcome. Let me introduce you to all the kids." Megan grabbed Kimmie's hand and took her to all the children. They surrounded her in no time.

Jena looked at her daughter's big smile and was so happy that she could be a real little girl for the first time. The running was finally over. Kimmie would get to have a childhood.

"How are you doing, Jena?" Doc Ryder came up beside her.

"I'm doing great. Never better."

"This must be your lovely mother," he said.

Sean put his arm around her mother. "Mom, this is our local doctor, Dustin Ryder."

"But everyone in town calls him Doc," Matt chimed in.

"These two set up an appointment for you tomorrow," the handsome doctor said to her mom. "I want to look at all your injuries to make sure you are healing properly. I got your records from Albuquerque this morning. I must say, knowing all you've been through, you look fantastic."

"It's the makeup, Doctor," her mom said with a wink.

Doc's brother came up with an older-looking gentleman with a distinct resemblance. Apparently the men in the Ryder family got a double dose of handsome genes.

"Mick, you remember Jena," Doc said.

"I do," the man said. "I'm sorry to interrupt, but my Uncle Gary wanted to meet you."

The Ryder's uncle took her mom's hand. "I'm so pleased to meet you, Mrs. Taylor."

"My name is Janet. May I call you Gary?"

"Of course you may. I would love to have a cup of coffee with you."

"I would like that," her mom said.

Jena could see the sparkle in her mother's eyes she hadn't seen in a very long time, and that made her happy.

"My nephews told me a little about what you did in New Mexico. I'm thrilled to meet such a strong, heroic woman."

"I'm sure you understand you would do anything for your children." Her mom pointed to Kimmie. "That little redheaded beauty is my granddaughter."

"Mom, Kimmie is having so much fun she doesn't know we're

here. Do you see that lady on the floor with all the kids?"

Her mother nodded. "She's got to be my age."

"Actually, she's quite a bit older, though you'd never know it. She's Gretchen, a fixture in Destiny and in the Knight's home."

"Who's the lady that is stacking all the presents?"

"That's Ethel, Mom," Matt told her. "She's the county judge."

"I'm sure you three will be good friends," Sean said.

"I hope we can be friends, too, Janet," the Ryder's uncle said with a smile.

"Let's see how the coffee date turns out first, Gary."

"Absolutely, but I'm glad you called it a 'date.' It gives this old man some hope."

As the party moved into full swing, Jena sat between Sean and Matt, watching Kimmie having the time of her life. All the children, including the early arrivals for the new boys' ranch Amber Stone was building with her three husbands, were playing with big smiles on their faces.

Kimmie ran up to her. "Mommy, Miss Gretchen said it was time to open my presents."

"She did?"

Her daughter smiled. "Have you ever seen so many?"

"No, baby." She gave Kimmie a big hug. "Never. Go open your presents."

Kimmie headed to the table with all her gifts, but before she got there, the arrival of a new group pulled her attention away. No wonder. Her daughter was crazy about animals. Two blind men, one was Caucasian and the other was African-American, walked into the ballroom with their guide dogs.

Jena intercepted Kimmie before she could touch the dogs. "Honey, I know you love puppies, but these are special dogs. They are the eyes for these two men."

"They have dog eyes?"

"Sort of," the handsome man with the dark chocolate skin

answered.

The other man nodded his head. "We can't see, so the dogs do our seeing for us. You can pet them if you like."

"Wow. What are their names?" Kimmie asked, petting the gentle German shepherds.

"Sorry, gentleman. My daughter is a bit excited today. This is her birthday party. I'm Jena Taylor, her mother."

"Pleased to meet you. I'm Jaris Simmons. This is my friend, Chance Reynolds and his dog Annie." He pulled out a gift from under his arm. "So this must be for Kimmie."

"For me?" her daughter said.

"Yes," Jaris patted his black German shepherd. "Sugar told me to bring you a present."

"Is it a puppy?"

"Kimmie, we talked about this already." She knew how badly her daughter wanted a pet but wasn't ready to spring that on Matt and Sean. They had already opened their home and hearts to her and her mom and Kimmie. "Be a good girl and put this with the others. It's time to open your presents anyway."

"Yeah." Kimmie ran over to the table where Gretchen, Ethel, and Jena's mom were waiting.

Finished with the unwrapping, Jena looked at the smile on Kimmie's face. She'd never been happier. "God, this is overwhelming, Megan. I'm not sure all of this will fit in the house."

Megan put her arm around her. "I know it's a lot, but after what you and Kimmie and your mom have been through, everyone in town wanted to make this birthday special."

"You did that and more."

"Jena, let Belle and me take away the empty boxes." Amber was glowing. Her baby was due next summer.

Belle held the bag and was already filling it with the discarded wrapping paper. Shane and Corey Blue were grabbing up more and handing it to her. Jena wasn't sure, but thought there might be some sparks happening between those three.

"Hold on, everyone," Matt announced. "May I have your attention."

Jena turned to him. "What's this all about?"

"You'll see," he told her. "Kimmie, come over here."

"Yes, Daddy." She skipped over to him and he bent down next to her and gave her a hug. "I want you to look over at the big door, baby. I think Daddy Sean will walk through with something special for you. Drum roll, please."

Everyone started hitting the table and stomping their feet to create the illusion of the sound.

Matt walked in, carrying a doghouse. "This is for my daughter, the birthday girl."

"What's that I hear?" Matt asked Kimmie. "There's something inside."

"A puppy. It's a puppy." Kimmie jumped up and ran to Sean.

He set the doghouse down and out came the cutest toy poodle puppy Jena had ever seen.

Kimmie squealed and all the kids came running to see her new pet.

Matt put his arm around her. "Look how happy Kimmie is."

"How did you know?"

"You learn a lot at a tea party on the back porch."

"What are you going to call your puppy?" Gretchen asked.

Kimmie held her poodle in her arms. "Her name is 'Happiness,' because this is my happiest birthday."

Jena felt her eyes well up. This was her happiest day, too.

Chapter Eighteen

"Wake up, sweetheart." Sean's voice jerked Jena from her sleep.

She lifted her head from the pillow and looked into his sexy eyes. "What time is it?"

"Time for some training," he answered.

"Training?" Her mind was a bit foggy, still feeling the warmth of her recent slumber. She was actually having trouble making sense of what he was saying. She yawned.

"Yes, we're going to start your training in the lifestyle."

"Where's Matt?"

"He went ahead to the club. We got Gold to open up early. Your first time at Phase Four needs to be private."

Coffee or not, her mind became sharp and alert. Matt and Sean were taking her to the club—*the club*. Phase Four. It took quite a lot of her willpower not to jump up and clap her hands together and scream how thrilled she was. That wouldn't be right. Best to keep the big bad Dom guessing some.

So, she shifted into a sitting position. "When do we start?"

The hint of a smile crossed Sean's face, but he remained serious and intense. "When I say, sub. Understand?"

"Yes, Sir," she answered, feeling excited and nervous at the same time.

Sean's entire outfit had one single hue—black. He wore a T-shirt, vest, jeans, and boots, each screaming of his dominant nature. God, he was pure, sexy manliness.

She resisted the urge to lick her lips. The role play of the other night had awakened overwhelming desire for more. Like then, her itch was once again coming to life, vibrating hot and deep inside her body. Recalling how she'd responded to him and Matt the other night, she needed her itch to be scratched so badly.

How far could she go in BDSM? *I'm about to find out, I bet.*

This class would open her up to Matt and Sean even more and to the lifestyle they enjoyed—at least that was what she thought it would do. Doubt began to crawl out from the back of the shadows of her mind. She wanted to please them. God knew they had pleased her and more. They'd already confessed their love to her and she to them.

"Time to get you cleaned up for the activities today." Sean lifted her off the bed and carried her into the bathroom. He had filled the tub with hot water while she was still sleeping. "Time to move you up a level, Jena. Things are about to get serious. He held her over the water and she could feel the steam hitting her naked backside. "We are in protocol now, sub. I expect you to listen to me and to follow my instructions. Understand?"

God, he is so intense right now. His masculinity blasted through her. "Yes, Sir."

"Good. We are going to test you, baby. That means we are going to push your limits. If you need to call out your safe word, Matt and I expect you to do it. Is that clear?"

She nodded.

"Very good." He lowered her into the water, which was hotter than she liked, and she liked a very hot bath. Of course, she wasn't about to complain or say "red" to him.

She reached for the sponge, but he grabbed her wrist, keeping her from getting it. "No."

"But I thought you said—"

Sean used his free hand to grab her nipple and pinch. The sting was sharp, delivering both a message of what he wanted—complete surrender—and a delicious bite that reached all the way through her body. He kept pinching, but let up on the pressure some, which only added to her growing desire. "While we are in a scene, like now, you have two things to focus on—pleasing me and Matt. That's all. Nothing else. If I wanted you to wash yourself, I would've told you. Understand?"

"Yes, Sir."

He released her nipple and wrist and grabbed the shampoo. "Dip your head down in the water."

It would take an hour to dry her long hair, but she wasn't about to argue. Instantly she took a deep breath and plunged into the tub as he'd commanded. Something told her that this was just a precursor of what was to come at the club. What in the world was Matt doing to make the place ready for her training? The thought sent a shiver through her even though she was sitting in hot water. Her skin was bright pink, but she was becoming accustomed to the temperature quickly.

When she came up, she saw him smiling, and that made her happy and warm. He washed her hair. It was luxurious and wonderful. Then he began tugging on her locks, gently at first and then harder.

"How does that feel, sub? You like when I pull on your hair, don't you?"

"Yes, Sir." Her cheeks got really warm.

"Baby, finding your hard boundaries, the things that will stop you, is what we're going to work on today. Does that surprise you?"

She was finding it hard to vocalize anything as he began strumming every inch of her body with the soapy sponge. "Yes, Sir. Honestly, I'm a little nervous."

"That's normal and actually a good thing. Matt and I will be able to use it to our advantage and to heighten your pleasure."

For the past several days and nights they'd already been providing her rapturous pleasure. They'd turned her life totally around in so many ways and so many places, including the bedroom. She'd never realized sex could reach such heights of absolute oblivion and joy.

Sean moved the sponge to her pussy, taking extra time there. "Any questions before I get you dressed?"

"Yes, Sir. What do you and Master Matt have in mind for me next? At the club, I mean? I'm no prude, but I'm inexperienced in this."

He laughed. "Darlin', you're going to find out so many things today. About yourself. About me and Matt. We're going to get you into a state of dreamy submission."

"What kind of…well, toys…will you use at the club on me?" She looked at him and was shocked to see him frown. *What did I do wrong?* Suddenly, she remembered. "On me, Sir?"

His lips turned up into the sweetest smile. "Don't worry, baby. We won't leave a single permanent mark on you for this lesson. But you will feel every bite long after we come back home." Sean cupped her chin. "This sub is nice and clean. Time to dry you off. Stand up."

Tingles spread through her as she rose to her feet. The hot water remained, lapping nearly to her knees. She shivered as the ambient air, which was much cooler than the water, hit her heated skin. Sean made her step out of the tub and dried her off thoroughly using several towels. Then he made her sit her bare butt on the sink counter. He plugged in a blow dryer and began working on her hair with a brush. His technique in styling her hair was a combination of gentle and rough.

"Have you ever heard or read about shibari?" he asked.

"No, Master." She was thrilled that he seemed willing to reveal at least some of what to expect at Phase Four. "What is that?"

He stroked her hair. "It's where Doms use special ropes on their subs. It came to us from Japan. Matt and I actually went there and worked with a master in the practice. It's quite beautiful. There are safety issues we will go over with you before we begin. Matt and I will each have two pairs of shears to cut the ropes should we need to. Do not hesitate to say your safe word if you need to, understand?"

"Yes, Sir."

As Sean continued to tell her about shibari, she imagined what it would be like to be bound in that fashion, completely dependent on him and Matt. A shiver ran up and down her spine. *This is just the verbal part of the lessons. Oh boy, oh boy!* Next, he would take her to Phase Four where she would get hands on—his and Matt's—training. She couldn't wait for the application part of the class. Her heart was fluttering in her chest like a humming bird.

She listened halfheartedly as her mind brought up all kinds of fantasies she would like to try with her two guys. Was that what this lifestyle was about? Exploration?

The depth of his experience in BDSM was heard in every syllable. Knowing that he and Matt were so skilled in the life made her feel even better about learning the ropes. *Learning the ropes?* She grinned, realizing that was exactly what was about to happen.

"...a lifelong journey of trust and discovery for us." Sean cupped her chin. "Are you taking this in?"

"Yes, Sir. I'm listening to every word."

He grinned wickedly, lightly pinching her nipples. "Prove it, sub. Tell me about shibari."

"I've been listening." She closed her eyes and ran through what he just told her. "Shibari is rope bondage from Japan. You and Matt went there and learned from a master. You have all kinds of ropes. Today, you will tie me up with some ones made of hemp that are dyed in a variety of colors. BDSM is about trust. It's a lifelong—"

He gave her a playful tweak on her taut buds. "Very good, pet. Very good indeed." He lifted her off the counter and to the floor. "Time to get you dressed."

The outfit he and Matt had decided on for this class was extremely provocative, even for her. A pink silky halter top that revealed a ton of cleavage held her breasts. He placed pink leather high heels on her feet that were stunning. She never shied away from a mini, but the strip of leather he put on her was shorter than any she'd ever tried before. No panties. *I'm brave, but oh my.*

"Your turn," he said, stepping back, clearly pleased with what he'd chosen for her.

"My turn, Sir?"

"You do the makeup. I will watch. I want to see the inner vixen in you come out, starting with your lips. This isn't about being conservative, baby. Go for it. Let your wicked side out. If the makeup isn't to my satisfaction, you will do it again. Understand?"

"I think so," she said, getting her bag. *If he wants me to look like a sex goddess, then that's what I will do.* She selected the hottest shade of red she owned. "Like this, Sir?"

He grinned broadly. "Exactly like that, sub."

After she finished with her face, she turned to him. He was still smiling, but there was something else in his face that got her tingling. Hunger.

They drove the short distance to Phase Four. The front door was locked, so he knocked. Matt answered the door.

"Fuck, she looks hot as hell." Matt's words pleased her. He was wearing the same type of leathers that Sean was. God, her two guys were sexy beasts. "Come on in. We're all set up and ready to go."

They walked into the club, which was empty.

"Take a long look, sub. This is special. Most of the time this place is busting at the seams." Sean led her past the reception desk and through a door that opened up to a large expansive area.

She saw four platforms acting as stages. On one was a lone cage. Another looked like a doctor's office. Next to it was an elevated space with odd-looking contraptions.

"This is the public area. We will get you on one of these stages one night to show you off."

They want to show me off. That made her excited, proud, and so deliciously nervous.

"Don't worry, baby," Matt said. "That's for later. But we wanted to get you in this big room alone so you can imagine what it will be like when we do put you up on a pedestal. What do you think about that?"

"If that's what you want for me, then I will try, Master."

"My God, you're making my dick hard already and we haven't even gotten started on your lessons."

"It'll be a few weeks before we unveil you, sweet sub," Sean said. "There are private rooms we'll be practicing in until then. Also, we want you to witness some scenes."

"I'd like that, Sir," she confessed.

"There are some amazing Doms and subs in this town. Some of the best we've ever seen, and Matt and I have seen many around the country and around the world."

"Let's get to it," Matt said, leading her up to the center stage. There was a metal chair with four tables around it. On the tables were ropes of several colors. The neat order of the shibari ropes impressed her. Matt and Sean had been trained by a Japanese master and were Masters in their own right. She trusted them with all her being.

Matt collected two of the green ropes and folded them in half in his hand. "These are for your gorgeous hair. They match your eyes. Touch them, baby."

With her fingers, she reached out to the green ties. They were beautiful and felt almost silky. She shivered, anxious to have them around her body.

"Get in the chair," he ordered.

She instantly obeyed. The mini was so short that she could feel the cold metal touch her ass. She looked out to the room. One day, there would be a crowd here of others also in the life. She would be center stage for them, for her two guys, for herself. Trembling, she closed her eyes, imagining what it would be like. Not too different than now. She was wonderfully nervous and deliciously dizzy. Her body was burning with anticipation.

Matt stroked her hair. "You did a good job, Sean. Not a single tangle."

"With her silky hair, it was no problem."

Matt came behind her, forming her hair into a ponytail. He wrapped the ropes around it, in and out. Sean walked to the side of the stage to a DJ booth. He punched a button and the room was filled with a lusty, tribal beat that vibrated on her skin.

"Don't forget your safe word, pet," Matt said.

"I won't, Master." But she had no intention of saying it. She saw that each of them had leather holsters for the shears that Sean had told her about. They were there as a safety measure only, but the way they wore them, one on each hip, reminded her of gunslingers. They were truly Texans, and she loved every inch of their ruggedness.

"Does this feel good?" Matt asked.

"Very good."

"This is setting you up for some bondage, too. A sub's hair is a tool that experienced Doms know how to utilize to add to a sub's pleasure. Hair bondage is just another way for me and Sean to control you." He jerked on her hair. "Understand?"

She nodded.

He traced his rough finger over her throat, sending a shaky sensation through her body. "Have you ever seen a prettier sub?"

"No. Never," Sean answered in a deep, hungry tone.

She felt moisture pooling between her thighs as Matt tugged on her hair, binding the red locks and green ropes together.

"We will use this to immobilize your head by attaching it to something, like this chair, or we can treat it like a leash, leading you around where we want you to go. Do what we want and the pulling will be light. Don't, and it will get harder. This is about submission—you surrendering everything to us."

She closed her eyes, realizing the depth of what she was doing with them. Surrendering wasn't something that came easy for her. For her whole life, she had to be strong. She was the one who held all the responsibility.

Letting go…is that what BDSM is all about?

Were these ropes only devices they used to help her get to a state where her mind could truly relax? She longed for that space, a space of true release where she could just be. No decisions. No worries. Just her and her Doms.

"Lesson one of shibari," Matt said, pulling gently on the ropes in her hair. "Stand up," he commanded.

She didn't resist. He and Sean were in charge, and she loved every second of it. Her body was warming with every tick of the clock.

"Your handiwork looks great, buddy," Sean said. "Those are the best knots I've ever seen you do."

"It's because of our sub, Sean. She makes it look beautiful," he answered, a big dose of pride in his voice. "Let's take off her clothes."

Matt and Sean stripped her out of her sub outfit—halter top, leather mini—but didn't remove the pink pumps from her feet. She'd always believed most men had a thing for women in high heels and now she was being proven right. Her guys liked her in stilettos.

Their hands wandered over her body shamelessly, and she loved every lingering touch. Never before had she felt so sexy, so wild, so free.

Matt took the remainder of the rope hanging down her back. "We're going to tie you up where your arms are locked behind you and your legs are bent until your heels press against your ass."

Sean held up a blindfold. "Can you picture that?"

"Yes, Sir," she answered, still standing in front of him. She was coming to realize that the game in the mind was part of the play, too.

He put the blindfold over her eyes, and the room disappeared. The thump of the drumbeat coming from the speakers vibrated on her skin.

Sean rubbed her ass and Matt her breasts. Electricity rolled through her body, sparking every nerve ending to life.

"Sub, what color state are you in?"

Touch me. I need to be touched. "I'm green, Sir."

She could feel them tie her wrists all the way up to her elbows behind her back, locking them to the ropes in her hair. It was only uncomfortable if she resisted, trying to pull them apart.

They both kissed her on the cheek. She felt totally vulnerable—totally safe.

"You're doing great, baby," Matt said.

"Amazing, for a first time," Sean added. "Do not hesitate to use your safe word, understand?"

"Yes, Sir." She was on fire. They wrapped her up in the ropes until she was completely immobile. She was completely theirs to do with what they wanted. God knew she loved them and wanted to make them proud. This lifestyle…their lifestyle…was her lifestyle now. This was the biggest lesson yet, and the sensations she felt were taking her to the moon. *This is what it means to really trust.*

"What is this?" Sean asked, placing something cold on her nipples, making her tingle.

"Is it ice, Sir?"

"Very good. What is this?"

She felt something soft on her abdomen that tickled. "I'm not sure. Is it a feather?"

"Right again."

Over and over, they continued the game of touching her naked body with something and making her guess. She missed a couple, but this part of the lesson wasn't about being right or wrong. It was about keeping her focus on her body, her desires, her sensations. They were sending her mind to the backseat so that she could experience, in every way, the pleasures they were giving her.

"What about this?" Matt asked.

She felt his fingers thread through her pussy's folds and she gasped, her need rising fast. "Oh, God, Master. Please. Please."

"Begging. Have you ever heard such sweet begging in your whole life, Sean?"

"No. Never. But I hope to hear more from our sweet sub's gorgeous lips for the rest of my life."

"Me, too," Matt agreed, licking her clit, sending her to the moon. "Me, too."

"Let's unwrap our sweetheart," Sean said. "I want to feel her pretty ass around my dick."

She could feel him applying lubricant to her anus, causing her to moan.

"And I want to feel her pussy around mine," Matt said. "Do you think you deserve that, sub?"

"Please, Master. Yes."

They untied her in a flash and gently rubbed the places the ropes had been on her body. They removed her blindfold. They were naked now, smiling, standing right in front of her, holding their erect, thick cocks. Sexy Doms. *I'm theirs and they are mine.*

Matt kissed her first, making her toes curl. "You did great, baby."

"I did, Master?"

"You did."

Sean stepped up and took his place. "You're a natural. God, we're going to have to step up our game, Matt, to keep ahead of this one. She's a fast learner." He bent down and devoured her lips. She was getting even wetter as the pressure continued to build inside her.

"Thank you, Sir." Her clit burned and ached until she was so dizzy she thought she might fall to the ground. No worries about that with her Tall Texan and Country Boy by her side.

Sean stretched out on the stage in front of her. "Lower her down on me backward."

Matt lifted her up in his arms and she wrapped hers around his neck. It felt good to feel his body on her skin. He bent down, skillfully placing her backside on top of Sean's frame. She felt the tip of Sean's cock at the tight entrance of her ass.

Sean grabbed her thighs. "Take a deep breath, sub."

She obeyed instantly.

"Let it out."

Again, she did as he'd commanded. When the last ounce of air left her lungs, she felt his cock enter her body. A quick sting and then nothing but want filled her entire being.

Matt gently pushed her so her back was to Sean's chest and crawled on top of her. Without hesitation, he shoved his cock all the way into her pussy.

Her guys thrust into her with perfect synchronization. She writhed between them, unable to still even a single inch of her body. Every part of her moved, vibrated, trembled.

"I'm yours." She moaned.

"Yes, you are, Jena," Matt said, his eyes locked on her.

"Every bit of you is ours," Sean whispered hotly in her ear. "Now and forever."

"She's close. I can tell."

"Come for us," Sean commanded.

Once again, she could not deny them anything. Their words, their touches, their love sent her over the edge and into much-needed release. "Yes. Yes. God, Yes."

Chapter Nineteen

Jena sat in the living room with the whole family. They'd seen Doc Ryder that morning after they'd returned from Phase Four, and she was thrilled with her mom's good report.

Jenna heard her mother's cell buzz. Now that she felt safe, it was so good to have real phones instead of burners.

Since her mother was still in her wrist braces, she answered it. "Hello?"

"Hello, is this Janet?" a man's voice asked.

"No this is her daughter. Who is this?"

"Hello, Jena. This is Gary Ryder. May I speak with your mother?"

"Please, hold on." She hit the mute button. "It's Mr. Ryder, Mom."

"I must've accidentally given him my number."

"You're actually going to try to sell us that story, Mom?" Sean asked with a laugh.

"Maybe."

"Accidentally…on purpose, you mean." Jena grinned. "Do you want to talk to him?"

"Put him on speaker, please."

Jena nodded and placed the phone next to her mother.

"Hello, Gary. This is Janet. I have you on speaker phone because of my injuries."

"Well, hello, lovely lady. I was wondering if you would like to have that coffee in about an hour at Blue's Diner."

"Blue's Diner. Where is that?"

"I thought perhaps your family could bring you to meet me until we get better acquainted."

Matt nodded that he would. Sean gave her two thumbs up.

"You are quite the gentleman, Gary. My family said that would be fine and I can tell they are hungry anyway."

"See you in an hour then."

"Okay. Bye."

Jena clicked off the phone. "Mom, you're going on a date."

"I know. That dear man must need glasses. Did you hear him call me lovely?"

"You are lovely," Matt said.

"I better go change my clothes and do the best I can to make myself presentable. Gary is quite charming, don't you think, Jena?"

"Very. Just like my guys. Want some help?"

"Sure. You can help me pick out what I'm going to wear."

* * * *

Matt sat at the table with Jena, Kimmie, and Sean. He was enjoying his delicious double cheeseburger and hand-cut fries. They were all keeping their eyes on the couple in the booth by the window—Mom and Gary Ryder.

"This was supposed to be a light lunch, bro." Sean shook his head.

"It is light."

"By your standards, anything less than half a side of beef is light."

"Kimmie, would you like some ice cream?" Alice asked, refilling all their drinks.

"Yes, please."

"Just one scoop," Jena said.

"Are you sure?" Alice asked. "If you are going to continue being a chaperone to your mother, you're not leaving any time soon. Your mom and Gary just asked for one slice of apple pie to share."

"Two scoops for Kimmie," Matt said. "And a slice of pie for each of us."

"Fine. I surrender to the majority."

"Good deal," Alice said. "It's on the house."

As she walked away, Jena smiled, turning her attention back to her mom's direction. "I haven't seen my mom this happy since dad passed away."

Sean put his arm around Jena. "I think we might be witnessing a love connection taking shape."

"Is Grandma going to get married?" Kimmie asked.

"We're getting ahead of ourselves, baby. This is only a first date," Jena said.

"Oh." Kimmie turned to him and Sean. "When are you going to marry my mommy, Daddies? I want to be your flower girl."

Jena's cheeks turned a beautiful shade of pink. "Kimmie Taylor, you don't ask those kinds of questions."

"Why not?" Matt asked, looking into the love of his life's green eyes. "I think it's a very appropriate question."

"Me, too," Sean agreed.

Being of the same mind, they both left their chairs and got down on their knees. He grabbed Jena's left hand and Sean her right.

"Jena Taylor, will you marry me?" he asked.

"And me?" Sean added.

"Yes, we will," Kimmie said, clapping her hands together.

Matt looked into her sweet, innocent face, and he knew his love for Kimmie was boundless. "Little one, me and Daddy Sean want you forever. You are our precious girl."

"Daddy Matt and I have talked about making you ours completely." Sean smiled. "We want to marry your mommy and adopt you."

"I will marry you." Jena squeezed their hands. "You've just made me the happiest woman in the world."

The diner's customers burst into applause. Mom and Gary came up together.

"Honey, this is wonderful," Jena's mother said.

"I know. I can't believe this."

Jason and Nicole, both in uniform, walked to their table. Nicole hugged Jena.

"Congratulations." Jason said. "How long before you tie the knot?"

"They just asked me, Sheriff," Jena said. "Unless you're Megan Knight, it takes time to plan a wedding."

As more Destonians in the diner came around the table to give their words of congratulations, Matt felt his heart warm. He loved this moment. It would be one he'd tell their children and grandchildren about. It was so right.

Looking over Sean's shoulder at the entrance, his gut tightened at the new arrival he saw. Niklaus Mitrofanov.

"Sean," he said in a tone he knew would get his friend's attention.

Reaching into his jacket for his gun, he saw Sean do the same.

Mitrofanov wasn't alone. Three men followed him. The group walked brazenly to their table.

Jason and Nicole stood up, blocking the mobster from moving forward. Jena's mom came up beside Mitrofanov, causing Matt's gut to tighten. She wasn't from Destiny, so she wouldn't recognize the Russian. Gary pulled her back and placed her behind him. He might stay out on his farm most of the time, but he was still a Destonian. He knew what the mobster looked like and how dangerous he could be.

"Back off, Sheriff," the bastard said. "I have my attorney with me, and we have every right to be here. You wouldn't arrest this thief, so I took another legal course available to me."

"What course is that?" Matt asked, his fingers still on his Glock. One wrong move and Mitrofanov would be sporting a bullet between his eyes.

"I am going to sue Jena Taylor, that's what." Niklaus held some papers up for the whole room to see.

"What in the world would you sue my daughter for?" Mom asked. "Who are you?"

"I am Niklaus Mitrofanov, madam. These documents will ensure I get my money back from this criminal."

"Who the hell are you calling a criminal?" Mom's face was hot.

Jena moved to her feet, putting her arm protectively around Kimmie. Her other hand was in her purse, obviously reaching for her pistol.

Matt loved the fire he saw in Jena and Mom, but now was not the time. "Honey, relax. Mom, let Sean and I handle this." He knew that once they got the laptop from Black, everything would turn to their favor. They were holding all the cards, not this fat, bald fuck.

Mitrofanov held the documents out to Jason. "Take these, Sheriff, and do your duty. Serve these papers to this woman."

"If anything needs to be served, have your attorney make an appointment with me." The anger on Jason's face couldn't be missed.

"You haven't heard the end of this, Sheriff," Mitrofanov said. "You must uphold the law."

"That's exactly what I intend to do," Jason shot back.

"Niklaus, I recommend we do as the sheriff says," the man next to him, clearly his attorney, said. "All you want is a day in court. I can assure you that will happen."

Mitrofanov glared at the entire crowd of Destonians who were ready to jump to Jena's defense at a moment's notice.

The mobster stormed out the door with his entourage.

When the door closed, everyone returned to their seats, except Mom and Gary and Jason and Nicole, who remained next to their table.

Alice brought over Kimmie's ice cream. "Honey, would you like to sit at the counter like a big girl with me? I think your mommy and daddies need to talk."

"Is it okay, Mommy?"

Jena nodded, keeping her hand in her purse and her stare at the door Mitrofanov had left through.

Alice led Kimmie to the counter. Matt watched as his daughter climbed up on the barstool and dug into her ice cream.

"Who the hell does that son of a bitch think he is coming into my town and threatening people?" Jason said. "Black told Dylan that he will be here with the laptop in a few hours."

"We need that evidence now," Nicole said.

"You're right about that," Jason agreed. "Once we have it in our possession, we'll see what Mitrofanov thinks about that. Even his high-dollar mafia attorney won't be able to help him."

Matt felt his cell vibrate. He pulled it out and read the text. "Dylan wants us all back at your office, Jason. Mr. Black is with him now."

"He came early," Nicole said.

"Mom," Jena said. "Do you mind staying here with Kimmie?"

"Not at all, honey."

Gary nodded, looking directly at him and Sean. "I'll stay with Janet and Kimmie, too."

He liked the guy more and more. "Thanks."

* * * *

Sean walked to the building that housed the jail and sheriff's office. Jena was between him and Matt. Jason and Nicole led the way in.

"They're already in your office, Sheriff," Shannon, Jason's admin, stated flatly.

They all walked past her, entering the room.

Facing each other, Dylan and Black sat in chairs. On the table between them was what he hoped would send Niklaus to prison. *A laptop.*

"We have all the goods on this we need," Dylan said. "Including things about your ex-boyfriend, Jena. We can get the money that vanished after your dad died back for you."

"How?"

"It's in the Caymans. All of it. Black says we can have it back in your mom's accounts in under three months. The Knights' money is there, too."

"Not all of it," Black told them. "Five million is still missing."

"I don't understand." Jena shook her head. "Mitrofanov had nothing to do with Carl."

"That's true, but Kip Lunceford did," Black told them. "Lunceford recruited you to bring down TBK. He also met with Mitrofanov."

"Lunceford is the common denominator in all this mess." Sean squeezed Jena's hand.

"Yes, he is," Black said. "With the lines of code you sent back to the Agency, we were able to decipher a ton of terrorist plots Lunceford is behind."

"It was Jena's code, boss," Matt said. "She's the one who figured out most of the algorithms that Kip had embedded into TBK."

"Perhaps I should recruit Jena," Black said, his tone more serious than Sean would like.

"Boss?" Jason's eyebrows shot up.

Jena turned to him and Matt. "Are you two still on the CIA's payroll?"

Sean looked at Black. The man nodded, giving him the green light to break his cover. "Yes, we are, honey."

"But the CIA isn't supposed to work on US soil," Jason pointed out.

Black leaned forward. "Technically we're not. But we're chasing an international cyber terrorist who happens to be based here. We're working closely with the FBI to bring this guy down."

"I don't understand," Megan said. "I thought you were working for TBK."

"That, too," Matt told her. "We were sent here because Lunceford's digital fingerprints have been showing up all around the world. Only Dylan knew. We had to remain undercover in case Lunceford had someone at the company in his back pocket like he once had in Felix Averson. We've never been able to connect the dots to Kip until now."

"You mean until her," Black pointed at Jena.

"She's not joining the Agency," Sean said firmly. *No way. No how.*

"But what a great asset she would be," Dylan said. "Black has a great plan that she would fit into."

"That coming from you is rich," Matt snapped. "You quit. You left the Agency."

"Yes, I did."

Black held up his hand. "I'm not here in Destiny just to deliver this laptop. Yes, this will give the sheriff all he needs so he can arrest Mitrofanov. That's a good thing. But I'm also here to get Dylan back on my team. Before you say anything, Dylan, hear me out."

Black told them all about a new team he was putting together to combat all kinds of international cyber terrorism. He wanted Sean and Matt on the team, with Dylan being the lead.

"Hold on, Mr. Black," Jena spoke up. "I'm one of the best. And my guys know it. I love this country. If I can help keep it safe, that's what I will do. I want to be on your team."

"I'm not going back to Langley," Dylan stated flatly.

Black shrugged. "I'm willing to let you stay here in Destiny. I'm sure I can work with Scott and Eric Knight. They already have contracts with the military. Getting another contract set up for the Agency won't be a problem."

"We'll need to secure some additional offices," Dylan said.

"Sounds like you're back in the fold," Black said with a smile.

"Maybe," he answered. "I want to talk to Erica and Cam first before I commit."

"What about me?" Jena asked. "Am I in or not?"

"Guys?" Black looked at him and Matt.

"I can't refuse her anything," Sean told him, putting his arm around her. "Besides, I would like having her at the office with us."

"No fieldwork for Jena, Black," Matt interjected. "That's a deal breaker. We have a five-year-old daughter to worry about."

"You've got a deal. I had this in mind and we've already finished her background check." Black turned to her. "Those gray areas of your past, which actually were quite noble in my opinion, have been cleaned up. Your record is spotless now." Black turned to Jason and Nicole and handed them a file. "This is from the governor of Colorado, who you eventually report to. Sheriff, you and your deputy are consultants to this new team now."

"That's unusual," Nicole said.

"Very. Kind of like this whole town." Black smiled. "Like I did with Miss Taylor, I ran background checks on both of you. You now have top security clearances."

"Hey, I like my job," Jason said. "I worked hard to get elected. I have no plans on leaving this desk now."

"You won't have to. I only need you to be available from time to time." Black sighed. "Lunceford is being moved, and that should shut off his reach. But his organization is broad. We need to get all the nodes he's set up and all his accomplices out of commission. Since Lunceford seems to be focused on your town, I would think you would want to play a part in doing that, too."

"I'm in. You sold me, Black. My town means everything to me."

"Me, too," Nicole said.

Ethel walked in. "Shannon called me." She turned to the sheriff. "Jason, I understand you have enough evidence for me to grant a warrant for Niklaus Mitrofanov's arrest."

"Yes," Jason said. "And I want to get on it immediately."

"Give me what you have and I will give you what you need if you have enough," Ethel said.

Black showed her the laptop and brought out some printed copies of e-mails that his team had extracted from it.

"Looks to be in order," she said. "I heard Mitrofanov is back in town."

"He is," Dylan said. "I'm ready to take down that asshole."

"Not alone," Black interjected. "He's not alone. Ever. We need a whole team."

"This is my town, Black. Not yours. I'm still in charge," Jason said. "But I agree. Dylan, Matt, Sean, and Black, raise your right hands. Repeat after me."

"Hold on," Jena said. "What about me? I have a gun."

"Yes, you do, dear, but I want you to stay with me. Let these men handle this," Ethel said in a tone that was commanding. "One thing I've learned over my life is to know when to let the men do their jobs."

"But I can take care of myself."

"Yes, I can see that. But you have Kimmie to think about, don't you?"

He could see that Ethel's words had turned Jena around, but her face showed concern. She looked at Matt and him. "Please be careful."

"Honey, don't worry," Matt told her. "We'll be right back with the scumbag."

"Now that that's settled, let me continue. Gentlemen, repeat after me. I do solemnly swear to…" As Jason continued with the oath that would deputize them, Sean looked at Jena. Lunceford was going to a cage that could hold him and Mitrofanov was about to get sent away for good.

He walked out of the sheriff's office with Matt and the other men.

Jena's nightmare was about to be completely over.

Chapter Twenty

Keeping his eyes on every window of the house, Matt followed Nicole and Jason up to Mitrofanov's front door.

They all had their guns out and Jason held the warrant in his free hand.

He steadied his breathing, scanning every direction for any movement.

Dylan, Sean, and Black had gone around back in case the mobster or any of his cohorts tried to escape.

Jason pounded on the door, and they all waited for it to open.

* * * *

Jena's heart was racing. *Please, God, take care of them.*

"Honey, your guys are very well trained," Ethel told her. "They'll be safe. You'll see. They know what they're doing."

"I know they do, but Mitrofanov is a monster." Her anxiety was at an all-time high, which was saying something given all she'd gone through.

She heard the door open in the exterior office where Shannon worked.

Surely, they aren't back already.

* * * *

Sean motioned silently to Dylan and Black that his side of the house was clear. No Russian mobsters.

Dylan gave the same signal about the other side.

They all aimed their guns at the back door in case the creep and his crew tried to run.

They wouldn't be going far.

* * * *

Jena's heart jumped up in her throat when she heard two men with Russian accents talking to Shannon from the other side of the door.

"We know she's here," one of them said.

Mitrofanov's men.

"You're wrong," Shannon lied. "Miss Taylor went to Phong's Wok twenty minutes ago."

She turned to Ethel, who already had her gun out. The woman held her index finger up to her lips. She nodded. No talking. Be quiet. She brought out her own gun from her purse, praying she wouldn't have to use it.

* * * *

Matt watched Jason pound on the door again. In his gut, he felt something was wrong. His instincts had never failed him in the field before. What was Mitrofanov up to?

Jason pointed to the door. "Time to bust this down."

"Let's try the doorknob first." Nicole turned it. "Unlocked."

The hairs on the back of his neck stood up.

Something is definitely wrong. But they had to keep moving forward. This was the mission.

Cautiously, they all walked into the house.

"This is Sheriff Wolfe," Jason shouted as they all scoped out the room. "I have a warrant for Niklaus Mitrofanov. Show yourselves. Don't do anything stupid."

No answer.

Nothing.

They walked through the place, staying alert.

"The bastard and his men are gone," Nicole said, holstering her weapon.

"Fuck," he said aloud. He looked at the coffee pot on the counter. It was half-full and still steaming. "We must've just missed the bastards."

"How many cameras does a mobster need?" Nicole shook her head. "They are all over this room."

"There were several outside, too," Matt added.

"Come on in, fellows," Jason yelled out a back window to Sean, Black, and Dylan.

"Matt, do you know what this is," Nicole said, motioning to something behind a chair.

He came around to get a better view of the device and instantly recognized it.

A bomb.

* * * *

"I'm telling you both, I'm the only one here." Shannon's voice came through the closed door to Jena's ears, fueling her already racing heartbeat.

Shannon might be in her sixties but she still had the fire of a twenty-year-old.

Jena turned to Ethel, aiming her gun at the door, ready to do whatever necessary should it come to the worst.

The women of Destiny were capable. Very capable. She thought of Megan, Nicole, Amber, Gretchen, Erica, and so many others, all of them wonderful examples for Kimmie.

Kimmie. Please, God, don't let me die here. I need to live for my baby.

"Let us see who is in the sheriff's private office," one of the

Russians said.

"You can't go in there," Shannon told them. "Stop or I will use this."

Jena heard a scuffle.

The bastard laughed. "You thought this pea shooter could stop me."

Two gunshots fired.

* * * *

Matt looked at the timer on the sophisticated bomb behind the chair.

There was enough Semtex, the Soviet's version of C4, to blow up the entire block.

The blue numbers showed less than five minutes until detonation.

"Everyone out. This is a bomb and it's about to blow. Get the neighbors far away."

Black ran up beside him as the rest raced out the door. "Go, Dixon. I can diffuse it."

He knew his boss had experience deactivating all kinds of explosives, but this clearly wasn't an ordinary device. "If you haven't done it in two minutes or less, get out of here."

"I will," Black said. "Go make sure all the civilians are safe."

* * * *

Jena saw the door open. Time seemed to slow to a crawl.

Tick. Tock. Tick. Tock.

Every shaky breath matched her racing pulse.

With her finger on the trigger, she watched the two thugs enter, their guns drawn.

They fired their guns in every direction, and she ducked behind a desk.

Ethel crouched down behind the sofa, unloading her bullets from her handgun.

Jena did the same, squeezing the trigger again and again, begging the heavens for a miracle.

"Bitch." The bigger of the two groaned and slumped to the ground.

The thinner man with the tats that ran up his neck turned to her.

Their eyes locked as he swung his weapon her direction.

She fired her gun and watched his eyes widen. He fell to the ground, his weapon still in his hand.

* * * *

Matt stood next to Dylan, across the street from Mitrofanov's house. Sean had already headed back to get Jena and tell her the news about Niklaus's disappearing act.

"Somehow, the man was tipped off that they we were coming," Dylan said.

"By whom? Shannon Day? Ethel? Neither seems likely to me, and everyone else that knew about the laptop and warrant is here."

"Not Jena," he said flatly. "She's not in on it, Dylan. I know her. She's innocent."

Dylan nodded. "That's good enough for me."

The block was mostly empty. Being the middle of the day, most Destonians were at work. Jason and Nicole had already led those who were at home on this street to a safe distance.

He looked at his watch. "Two minutes have passed since we exited the house."

Dylan nodded. "That leaves three until the bomb detonates. Black needs to be getting out soon."

"We both know him. He'll get it done. He's the best."

"Yes, he is."

Dylan clearly admired Black as much as he and Sean did. Black wasn't just their boss. He was also a mentor and a friend.

He felt his cell buzz, indicating he'd gotten a text message.

Was it from Black?

"I got one, too," Dylan said, taking out his phone.

Matt pulled out his cell and what he saw made his heart freeze.

Out of the corner of his eye he saw Jason and Nicole running his direction and waving their arms. Each held their cells in their hands.

They'd gotten the same message:

This is Kip Lunceford, Destonians.
Time is a funny thing.
How often do you think you have more time than you have?
What time is it?
It's time to learn a lesson in humility.
Boom!

He and Dylan started to run into Mitrofanov's house. He opened his mouth to yell to Black to get out, but he was too late.

The bomb exploded, its deafening sound spreading faster than the debris.

He and Dylan rolled to the ground behind a car parked in the street.

His mind went back to the day, years ago, when he and Sean had emerged from the tunnel away from the burning compound of the cult. Sean's and his parents had died that day. *My little sister, too.*

Peeking over the car, he saw the flames licking the shell of the house that Black had been inside.

He knew his boss—his friend—had just been murdered by a madman.

* * * *

Jena shivered violently, realizing the gravity of what had just happened.

The two thugs remained on the floor. Keeping her gun ready, she leaned forward, listening for any sound from the duo. Nothing. Not even a gasp or moan. They were dead.

"We did it, Ethel." She'd gotten her miracle, thank God.

"Jena, check on Shannon," the woman said from behind the couch.

"On it." She ran out the door.

Jena knelt down by Shannon, who was on the floor. A large dark stain on her blouse revealed she'd been shot, her pink wig askew and her eyes glassy.

Jena put her finger to Shannon's neck. No pulse. She saw another wound, this one in her temple, half-hidden by her wig, and she knew Shannon was gone.

Tears filled her eyes, staring down at the brave woman's body.

She ran back into Jason's office, stepping over the two dead Russians. "Where are you?"

"Over here," Ethel choked out.

The sound of the dear lady's voice told Jena something was dreadfully wrong. When she got to Ethel, she saw the woman had been shot.

Chapter Twenty-One

Jena looked at Ethel's leg, which was bleeding. Standing up, she grabbed the scissors from Jason's desk.

"What are you doing?" Ethel asked, her face pale and her lips quivering.

"Making a tourniquet." She pulled off her top and cut it into strips.

Sean ran into the room, and she felt the weight on her shoulders lighten some. *He's safe.*

"Matt?"

"He's fine." He took the strips and bent down over Ethel. "I've got this, baby. Call Doc Ryder."

She nodded, jumping to the phone.

In a flash, he had Ethel's wound taken care of. "Field dressing is something I'm familiar with."

"Apparently so," the woman said, her words coming out slurred.

"Ethel, you've lost some blood but not too much. You're going to be fine."

"I know." She laughed weakly. "This old woman is too tough to go out by two chicken-shit mobsters."

"Doctor Ryder's office," said a voice over the phone. "This is Nurse Cottrell. How may I help you?"

She recognized the woman's voice. "Paris, this is Jena Taylor. We need Doc at the sheriff's office now. There's been a shooting."

* * * *

The next day, Jena stood between Matt and Sean, waiting for their turn to see Ethel. Gretchen was in front of them, the next to be allowed in. The line outside Ethel's room was extremely long. No surprise. All of Destiny had shown up to see their favorite judge.

Doc Ryder and Paris stood at the door, monitoring to make sure everyone abided by the rules of no more than three visitors at a time.

The Knights came out together.

"How is she?" Gretchen asked the trio.

Megan wiped her eyes.

"She's tough, Gretchen," Scott answered.

Eric nodded his agreement. "Tough as nails."

The dear lady grabbed Megan's hands "I know. Like you."

"And you," Megan said.

Gretchen smiled and walked into the room. Doc Ryder closed the door and crossed his arms over his chest. He was serious about the number of visitors he was letting in at a time.

Megan stepped in front of Jena. "You were so brave."

She shrugged. "Not really. I did what I had to do."

"More than that, I know." Megan turned to Matt and Sean. "I'm so sorry about Mr. Black. This is all my fault."

"You have nothing to be sorry about," Matt said kindly.

Jena could see the pain on his and Sean's faces about Black.

Sean sighed. "These are Kip's and Mitrofanov's crimes. Not yours, Megan."

"But he's *my* ex. What if I'm the reason he's doing all of this?"

"Sweetheart, don't," Eric pleaded, holding her close.

Scott kissed her cheek. "Baby, Lunceford is insane. Who knows why he does what he does?"

Jena squeezed Megan's hands again. "The creep is going away for good. Your ex will not be able to hurt you or anyone else ever again. We will also find Mitrofanov and send him to a cage that he will never get out of."

"I hope so," Megan said. "But Kip is brilliant. Who would've thought that he had a wiretap on Jason's office? A camera at Mitrofanov's house? Shannon is dead. Black is dead. There is blood on my hands."

Jena put her arms around Megan. "What happened at the sheriff's office is Mitrofanov's and Kip's doing. They will pay for Black's and Shannon's murders. You had nothing to do with it."

Trying to discover how Mitrofanov had known to skip town right after the warrant had been filed, Dylan had uncovered the wiretap on the sheriff's landline. Shannon's call to Ethel to come over had clearly tipped Kip off. He must've contacted the mobster immediately. The bomb had been activated. Nicole had reminded everyone about the cameras she'd seen at Mitrofanov's house. They all believed that Kip must've been watching when Black was trying to dismantle the bomb. That's when he'd sent the text message to every phone in Destiny. Then remotely, he'd detonated the deadly thing early, killing Black.

"Shannon's funeral is tomorrow," Megan said. "I just can't believe she's really gone. And poor Mr. Black. What kind of memorial can his family have? His body still hasn't been found, has it?"

"The detectives are still going through the rubble, but so far, no." Sean sighed. "No cameras have been uncovered at the crime scene either."

"True," Matt said. "But additional investigating has discovered bugs, wiretaps, and spy cameras all around Destiny."

Shockingly, the whole town had been under Lunceford's digital microscope for some time.

Even if Kip was about to be put in a box and wouldn't have access to the information himself, one of his cronies might be holed up in some warehouse, like she had been in Odessa not that long ago. No one wanted to be monitored by some unseen enemy.

Megan shook her head. "I can't believe that bastard has been watching and listening to all of us."

"He has, but he won't for long." This was Jena's town now, too. She was determined to help bring down the son of a bitch. "Matt, Sean, Dylan, and I are working to disable all Lunceford's detection devices in Destiny. We will take away his eyes and ears."

"I'm glad, but can't you understand why I feel so responsible?" Megan asked.

She nodded. "For years I carried guilt for things I had no control over. My dad's death. The loss of my family's money. Having to run with Kimmie and my mom. None of it was my doing. It was Carl's, just like this is Kip's."

"Thank you, Jena. That helps. I will feel better when he's at the new prison."

"We all will. Day after tomorrow," Matt said. "Until then, he'll be under constant watch."

"The next group may go in," Doc said.

"That's you and your guys," Megan said to her. "Ethel will be glad to see you, and I'm sure Patrick and Sam will be, too."

She hugged her friend again before walking into Ethel's room with Matt and Sean.

Entering, Jena saw Patrick and Sam O'Leary on either side of their wife. Ethel was in the bed sitting up, looking as beautiful as could be.

"There's the real hero." Ethel motioned her closer. "How are you doing, Jena?"

"Better than you."

"Don't bury me yet. I might be down for a day or two but I'm definitely not out. Besides, I have to prepare for the annual Halloween Party at our home."

"Darlin', that event is in less than four days." Sam frowned. "You cannot pull that off even with Patrick's and my help."

"If we have to postpone, then that's what we'll do. Your health is more important to us," Patrick pointed to the center of his chest and then at Sam, his brother. "Who cares about some old party when it comes to you?"

"Old party? Patrick Michael O'Leary, you listen to me. We are having our party on Halloween, not some later date. I will be up and out of here by tomorrow. Doc Ryder said so. Gretchen, Megan, and the others told me they would help." She grabbed Patrick by the hand. "Besides, I will not be the cause of disappointment for our neighbors. Everyone loves hearing your speech."

"Speech?" Jena asked. "At the party?"

"Yes, dear," Ethel answered. "It's a tradition. Every Halloween, Patrick gets up and tells the tale of how he met his first dragon when he was a prisoner of war in North Korea for seven months."

Her mouth dropped. "Patrick, you were a POW?"

He shrugged. "I wouldn't have met my first dragon had I not been."

Ethel reached up and lovingly touched his face. "And during Dragon Week in March, he actually gives lectures. Several of them."

"And attendees get to hear about my brother's treks to Scotland, Peru, Arkansas, and elsewhere—each having their own reported dragon sightings." Sam rolled his eyes. "I still can't believe him. If it wasn't a hallucination, then what could it be? Nothing physical, that's for sure. Something that big would've made a noise or at least have been seen by more than just a few people."

"Lots of people have seen the Loch Ness Monster, which we all know is actually a sea dragon. You are such a skeptic, Sam. I saw it. I wasn't on drugs. I was in my right mind."

Jena couldn't help but giggle. It was clear these two had been arguing about this for decades, with neither one conceding a single inch to the other.

"No more, I tell you," Ethel said with a smile. "We have guests. Jena, how is Kimmie doing?"

"She's great." She turned to Sam, who was a semi-retired psychologist. "Thank you for setting up those sessions with her and my mom."

"And you," he said. "What you went through in Albuquerque was awful. What happened at the sheriff's office only compounded more issues we should go through."

"Stop pedaling your mumbo-jumbo to Jena," Patrick teased. "There's plenty of time for that."

The bond between the O'Leary brothers was firm and clearly unbreakable. After more than eighty years, that was saying something.

Being an only child had been difficult in some ways for Jena. She wanted Kimmie to have siblings. She turned to Matt and Sean, knowing they would love to have more kids, too. Life was good.

"I do want to come see you, Sam. I think it will be good for Kimmie and my mom, too."

"Word on the street is your mom and Gary Ryder have a budding romance going," Ethel said.

"That's putting it mildly," Matt said.

Jena grinned. "They are never apart, if that's any indication."

"That's great," Patrick said. "Gary is a good man. His wife died years ago. It's time he got his happily ever after."

She nodded, glad that her mom and Gary had found each other.

Paris opened the door. "Doctor Ryder says your time is up. The line has doubled since you came in."

"Tell him to relax. I'm the patient. I love seeing my friends. It's the best medicine a woman could ask for. Jena, be sure to bring Kimmie and your mom to the party."

"I will."

"What about us?" Matt teased. "Sean and I are still invited, too, aren't we?"

"It wouldn't be a party without Destiny's favorite Texans," Sam said.

"We'll be there," Sean said.

"In costume," Patrick demanded.

"Yes, in costume. All of us," Jena answered. "I'm not sure what, but I bet Megan can help me pull something together."

* * * *

Jena walked into the O'Leary mansion with Kimmie and her two wonderful men. Her mom and Gary had come earlier. She couldn't wait to see what the happy couple had chosen to come as. Her mom had been so secretive about it, dressing at the Knight Mansion instead of back home.

The place was decked out in a whimsical version of Halloween. More fun than scary, though she'd been told that the basement had been turned into a haunted house for the older kids and adults.

"You look amazing," Megan said, running up to her. "I told you that Robin Hood and her Merry Men would be a hit. Look at all the smiles." She pointed to the loving Destonians around the space turning around, smiling and giving them their nods of approval.

"I couldn't have done it without you." She hugged her friend.

Megan bent down and hugged Kimmie. "You are the prettiest Maid Marion I've ever seen."

Kimmie kissed her on the cheek. "Thank you, Aunt Megan."

"Oh my," Megan said. "Who told you to call me that, baby? I love it."

"My mommy said it would be okay. Is it okay with you?"

She hugged her again. "More than okay, Kimmie. You're going to have a little cousin before too long to play with."

"A girl cousin, right?"

Megan smiled. "Maybe. I hope she's as pretty as you."

"Me, too. No boys. They're not pretty."

"One day you'll change your mind about that, I bet. But until then, I've got my fingers crossed for a little girl, too."

Kimmie held up her hands and crossed her fingers. "Me, too, Aunt Megan."

Jena's mom and Gary came up beside her dressed as Cleopatra

and Marc Antony. "Honey, you look so cute," she told Kimmie. "All of you do. Gary, what do you think of our family?"

"Sean makes a pretty good Friar Tuck." Gary turned to Matt. "Are you Little John."

"That's what I'm trying to pull off."

"You nailed it." Gary bent down. "But none of you hold a candle to Maid Marion. Kimmie is the best."

"Yes, she is," Sean and Matt said in unison.

Matt smiled. "Robin Hood is quite beautiful, too."

"Prettiest version of the thief I've ever seen," the man said.

"Cleopatra isn't bad either," Sean added.

"I agree with you about that," Gary said, pulling her mom in close.

Ethel stood on the stairs. She was regally dressed as a queen. "Everyone, it's time to go into the ballroom for Patrick's tale about his first dragon sighting."

As the crowd shuffled ahead, Megan took Kimmie's hand. Her mom took Gary's.

Jena stood between Friar Tuck and Little John, who she'd first known as Country Boy and Tall Texan.

So much had changed since then. No more running. Ever.

Matt grabbed her hand and Sean put his arm around her. They led her into the room where Patrick was about to give his speech. She'd fallen for the whole town from the first day they'd all welcomed her with flowers. Destiny was a place where judgment was left outside the city limits. The only rule of family was love. Here, a woman could find happiness in the arms of two amazing Texans.

Jena smiled, knowing she would spend the rest of her life in this quirky town with Kimmie, her mom, and the two loves of her life, Matt and Sean. She'd finally come home.

THE END

WWW.CHLOELANG.COM

ABOUT THE AUTHOR

Chloe Lang began devouring romance novels during summers between college semesters as a respite to the rigors of her studies. Soon, her lifelong addiction was born, and to this day, she typically reads three or four books every week.

For years, the very shy Chloe tried her hand at writing romance stories, but shared them with no one. After many months of prodding by an author friend, Sophie Oak, she finally relented and let Sophie read one. As the prodding turned to gentle shoves, Chloe ultimately did submit something to Siren-BookStrand. The thrill of a life happened for her when she got the word that her book would be published.

For all titles by Chloe Lang, please visit
www.bookstrand.com/chloe-lang

Siren Publishing, Inc.
www.SirenPublishing.com